SPECIAL MESSAGE TO READERS

THE ULVERSCROFT FOUNDATION
(registered UK charity number 264873)

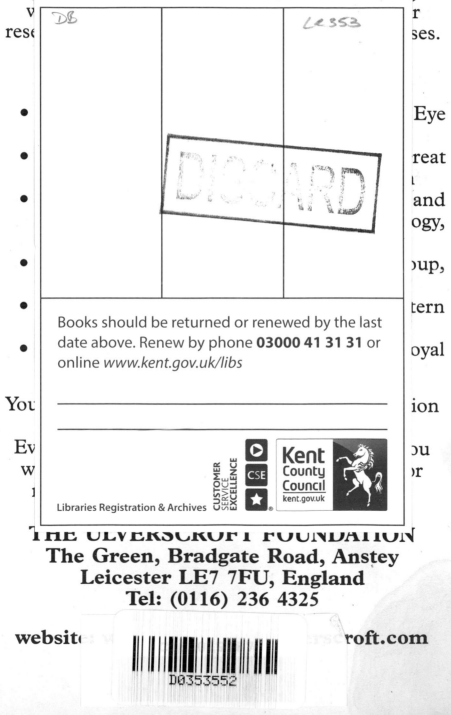

... r
rese ... ses.

- ... Eye
- ... reat
- ... and ogy,
- ... up,
- ... tern
- ... oyal

You ... ion

Ev ... ou
w ... or

THE ULVERSCROFT FOUNDATION
The Green, Bradgate Road, Anstey
Leicester LE7 7FU, England
Tel: (0116) 236 4325

websit ... roft.com

Susan Bridge is married with four grown-up children. She lives in rural Sussex with her husband, dogs and a large garden. Susan loves to travel: she enjoys trekking in the Himalayas, and has also developed a taste for white-water rafting.

SECRET INHERITANCE

When Dorothea Harcourt falls in love with the dashing Mr Detherfield she tries desperately to hide her feelings, afraid that he will uncover the scandal of her mother's past. Her problems multiply when the spiteful Mrs Howard threatens to reveal the secret, for exposure would ruin her cousin Clio's chances of marrying with an unsullied reputation. But when Clio is kidnapped and held for ransom, Dorothea must forget her old anxieties. She needs Mr Detherfield's help if she is to rescue her cousin before it is too late . . .

S. R. BRIDGE

◆

SECRET INHERITANCE

Complete and Unabridged

ULVERSCROFT
Leicester

First published in Great Britain in 2009 by
Robert Hale Limited
London

First Large Print Edition
published 2015
by arrangement with
Robert Hale Limited
London

A catalogue record for this book is available
from the British Library.

ISBN 978–1–4448–2504–6

Published by
F. A. Thorpe (Publishing)
Anstey, Leicestershire

Set by Words & Graphics Ltd.
Anstey, Leicestershire
Printed and bound in Great Britain by
T. J. International Ltd., Padstow, Cornwall

This book is printed on acid-free paper

1

The large parlour of the Old Bath Hotel in Matlock was almost empty. Only a group of three ladies sat by the window. The oldest of these looked around her rather sadly and sighed as she patted the lace cap on her grey curls.

'When your dear papa and I first came here to Matlock Bath ten years ago there was such a delightful company of people gathered. The assembly rooms were new and attracted such genteel ladies and their gentlemen escorts were far above those we have met since we arrived here a week ago.'

'Well, I did tell you we should go to Buxton at the very least,' complained the youngest of the three, a girl of about seventeen. She was exceedingly pretty with golden curls caught up with green ribbon and she was wearing a simple white-muslin dress trimmed with the same ribbons, which showed off her youthful slenderness to great advantage. Her small mouth was spoiled by a pout at that moment, but her normally sunny disposition made her a pleasant companion.

The third member of the trio was older

1

than her young relative — a few years and, at first glance, far less beautiful. Her face was oval in shape and lacked distinction until one studied her fine grey eyes fringed with very long dark lashes. Her normally serene expression changed as she listened and she hastened to intervene to prevent an argument.

'Now, Clio, you know we have been through all that on several occasions. Your mama considered Matlock far more suitable and since you are not yet out I think she was quite correct. It may be a little dull here but at least the surroundings are beautiful and the waters will do Aunt Sophie just as much good as those in Buxton.'

The older lady, Mrs Sophie Harcourt, patted her niece's hand gratefully. 'Thank you, Dorothea. I knew you understood when I first suggested we visit here, but Clio has her head stuffed full of romantic notions.'

'Well, Mama, you must admit that the gentlemen we have met so far have all been either too old or too infirm to even notice me, let alone Dottie. As she is paying for our trip it seems very unfair.' She got to her feet and flounced across the room to gaze out at the view of the River Derwent in the valley below.

Dorothea made to get up and follow her young cousin but Mrs Harcourt held her hand. 'Let her be, Dorothea my dear. She is so young it is only natural that she wants to be seen with handsome young gentlemen but I'm sure the next assembly will not be as dull as the one we attended here last night. She doesn't mean to be ungrateful you know.'

'Of course I know that, Aunt. I only wish you had let me take you all to Buxton or even to Brighton, which is so fashionable now in the summer months. I would have been delighted to do so.'

'You are the most generous girl but I couldn't let you spend all your little inheritance on us like that. You must save something for a dowry, you know.'

Dorothea laughed. 'I am unlikely to marry now, Aunt Sophie, and I would rather spend the money on your health since you have cared for me all these years. You are like a mother to me as well you know, and dear Clio is so pretty she should have a chance to meet fashionable young men.'

'I agree. I wish she could meet more suitable gentlemen but I fear it is beyond our means to go to London and take a lease on a house for the season, let alone meet the necessary expenses on clothes and entertaining. If your dear uncle had been alive maybe it would have been possible but I can see little hope since he passed away and left us.'

Used to such little outbursts, Dorothea helped her aunt find her handkerchief and waited patiently while that lady dabbed ineffectually at her dry eyes with the wisp of lace. Mrs Harcourt had been fond enough of her Edward but, apart from missing the income he provided, she was content enough with the two girls. However she knew what was expected of a widow of only three summers.

'I should like to use what money I have for Clio's entry into the fashionable world, Aunt Sophie. I really mean that,' Dorothea murmured as the handkerchief was tucked back into the lady's reticule.

'Nonsense. I cannot possibly permit you to do so,' Sophie Harcourt said stoutly, but she sighed at the idea and Dorothea hid a smile. She was certain she could persuade her relative in time. 'After all, you did sell your little house to help our income and you have brought us here. So kind,' Sophie murmured. 'Mind you, perhaps we should have gone to Bath as it's so genteel.' She loved the sound of this word and used it frequently. 'Still, this is a pretty place, as I said to Clio.'

'It is indeed. And you must forget my house. I had no need of it since you have always allowed me to call your home my own. It was much more sensible to spend the money as we have done. Say no more about it.'

'Oh dear!' exclaimed the widow dramatically and clutched Dorothea's arm. Her lavender-silk skirts rustled in agitation as she discreetly pointed to a new arrival in the room. 'Look! There is that dreadful Mrs Howard! She is so very vulgar and Clio will talk to her. She is doing so now. Oh call her for me, Dottie.' In her distress she used the old childhood name for her niece.

Dorothea got to her feet and moved across to place an arm on Clio's shoulder. She smiled at Mrs Howard who smiled back archly. The lady was dressed in a very smart afternoon dress of blue crêpe embellished with black ribbons, but with too much jewellery and a striped shawl over her shoulders, which spoiled the fashionable effect. She had on a tiny blue hat with black feathers on top of her elaborately dressed fair hair and was clearly intent on keeping Clio by her side.

'Your mother wants you to help her to her room for a rest,' Dorothea told the girl quickly. 'She is feeling tired.'

'Oh, what a shame. Just as I had asked the little dear to come for a walk with me,' Mrs Howard said cheerfully. 'Never mind. Another time, Clio.'

'I shall look forward to it,' Clio replied with a pretty show of manners. As she walked back to her mother's chair she gave Dorothea an impish smile. 'I'm glad you rescued me, Dottie. I had no desire to walk to the wishing well with her for I cannot really like her. I don't know why, though.'

'She tries too hard to please,' Dorothea told her sensibly. 'But do you want to go for a walk? I thought I would take a stroll up Matlock Dale and blow away the cobwebs.'

Clio shook her blond head and her curls bobbed. 'Oh no. I think I will rest like Mama. You go on, Dottie, while I take Mama upstairs. We will see you before dinner.'

Glad to get out at last Dorothea adjusted a shawl over her plain brown-wool dress. She had worn sensible shoes and no hat for there was quite a stiff breeze blowing on this September afternoon. It was wonderful to be free but she had a guilty qualm when she thought of her trusting Aunt Sophie. How could she, Dorothea, chastise Clio if she went off alone when she had sneaked out of the hotel without her maid? It was hopeless to have Annie with her though, for the girl hated walking and could only manage a few yards without beginning to trail behind.

There was a great deal Dorothea had to think about. As she wandered along the dry

6

and dusty road to Comerford the High Tor rose in front of her, a sheer wooded slope with grey limestone rock showing above the trees. It was stark and beautiful, just fitting her mood. Here on this lonely stretch of road she had left behind the elderly visitors to the spa and the few fashionables who preferred to wander the lovers' walks above the river.

The conversation she had just had with her dear Aunt Sophie had made her feel very guilty. Mrs Harcourt imagined that Dorothea had very little money and that in order to help the family after her uncle's death she had sold off her small inheritance. In a way this was true, except that Dorothea had not received a small inheritance. Only the year before, on her twenty-first birthday, she had been summoned to the lawyer's office in London to learn her good fortune. It had been her first visit to the capital and she had been both stunned by the size and sheer noise, yet excited by the bustle and life of the city. In the quiet seclusion of the lawyer's chambers he had informed her that the mother she had mourned as dead since she had been a small girl had in fact only recently died and had left a fortune to her daughter. Dorothea had been brought up in her aunt and uncle's household since her mother's apparent demise, as her father, a military man, was away too often to care for her properly. He had died when she was twelve; she had believed herself an orphan and loved her aunt as a mother. Clio was like a young sister to her and the girl's welfare was all-important to Dorothea.

She had been so stunned by the lawyer's revelations which, he stressed, were to remain confidential if she wished to keep an unsullied reputation, that as yet she had still hardly come to terms with her wealth. However, the secrecy surrounding her mother's lifestyle and last will and testament precluded Dorothea from taking her aunt into her confidence. She had been forced to resort to stratagems, such as the one about selling her house, to account for the money available for their visit to the spa.

She sighed as she wandered round a bend in the road. It was very difficult keeping the secret, yet she had no wish for anyone to know the truth either. She was so absorbed in her thoughts that she did not notice the approach of a light sporting curricle drawn by matched bays. It was almost upon her before she was aware of it and in her haste to move out of the way of the pounding hoofs she ran to the side of the road, tripped over her dangling shawl, and ended up in a heap on the bank. The vehicle narrowly avoided her slim ankles, which were clearly exposed to the view of the driver.

He reined in his team with skill and drew up. After throwing the reins to a groom perched behind he came back to assist Dorothea to her feet.

Instead of commiserating or asking after her health, he offered her a hand to get up and berated her. 'How stupid of you to be wandering down the middle of the road! You could have been killed or badly hurt, to say nothing of the possible damage to my horses,' he exploded.

Incensed at such lack of consideration and feeling rather more shaken than she cared to admit, Dorothea ignored his hand and quickly pulled her skirts down around her ankles. In spite of his fury the tall, dark-haired man gazing down at her had been studying her with open admiration, and a certain insolence too. 'It was entirely your fault,' she stormed at him. 'If you drive your horses at such reckless speeds it is no wonder ordinary citizens have to seek the shelter of the ditches!'

He frowned down at her. 'I was not to blame. A witless woman wandering the road deserves all she gets,' he snapped. 'Are you hurt?'

Struggling to her feet and finding herself shaking Dorothea answered him equally crossly. 'No, I am not, but that is no thanks to you. And how dare you speak to me in that tone.'

'Oh. And how should I address you, miss?'

Knowing that her hair had come unpinned and was tumbling over her shoulders while the offending shawl was still on the ground and was now filthy, Dorothea bit back another furious retort. She hardly looked like a lady, it was true, and since she was alone and consequently guilty of impropriety it was better not to admit her identity. 'I merely wished to express my annoyance at your disregard for other road users, and I am not a witless woman,' she told him as she bent to pick up her shawl.

He was before her and handed her the dirty object with lazy grace as if he was passing a lady a fan in a ballroom. 'I am sorry if I misjudged you, but by your appearance I took you for a farm girl on the way home from market. As you have no basket I must be mistaken.'

'You are indeed, sir.' Staring up at him, Dorothea saw he was now amused by her fury and that curiosity gleamed in the dark eyes regarding her. He was a very handsome man, she saw to her chagrin. Just the man she would have loved to meet in other circumstances and even with his dark hair blown by the wind under the curly beaver hat, his clothes and attitude showed him to be a gentleman. Her own knowledge that she had been dreaming and so deserved censure made her even more annoyed. When he had the temerity to chuck her under the chin and laugh kindly she could have hit him.

'Well, you are a little termagant whoever you are, but such disarray suits you. Can I take you for a ride now that I have spoiled your walk?'

The easy familiarity with which he addressed her made her heart sink. He considered her no lady and, alone as she was, it was not surprising. 'Your remarks are improper and impolite in a gentleman,' she told him, trying to sound dignified. 'I can walk back to Matlock Bath, I thank you.'

'Oho, independent are we? Well I am sure you can walk back but after such a fall it would be more sensible to accept a lift from me,' he said in a kindly and patronizing tone. 'Don't be foolish, young lady.'

'I cannot ride with strangers,' she objected at once, hot colour flooding her cheeks.

'I see I have been mistaken in thinking you a local girl and for that I apologize,' he told her quickly, sweeping off his hat and bowing slightly. 'Let me introduce myself. I am Martin Detherfield, and since I am on my way through Matlock it will give me great pleasure to offer you a lift there. Also, as my groom is with me the proprieties are nicely observed.' He added this last remark with a slight smile that made Dorothea blush even more.

'Thank you sir,' she said quietly. 'Then I accept your offer. It is not so far.'

'Can you walk?' he asked, real concern in his voice now as she staggered slightly. 'Let me assist you.'

Dorothea objected, but he placed an arm under her elbow and guided her to the curricle, where he handed her up into the seat. Knowing she was again showing her ankles made Dorothea wish that she had refused the ride, for this was not the type of carriage for a lady and she had never before sat in one. Martin Detherfield jumped up to sit beside her and gathered the reins in capable hands. The groom let the horses' heads go and leapt up behind as the curricle moved off.

'Now perhaps you would tell me your name?' Detherfield enquired. 'After such a stormy introduction I should at least know who you are.'

'Miss Harcourt,' she said without thinking.

'And where are you staying? At the Old Bath Hotel?'

Not wishing to give further information to this man and embarrassed now by the whole incident Dorothea ignored his question. Instead she pointed to the High Tor. 'Is it not beautiful, Mr Detherfield? I came out to admire the views and that is why you found me dreaming along the road. This part of Derbyshire is very lovely. Do you live near here?'

'Not too far away,' he told her. 'I am very fond of the area too and I am glad you admire the scenery. Do you take the waters?'

'No indeed. My aunt is doing so and they seem very beneficial,' Dorothea answered him.

'I see. So you are a companion to an elderly aunt and no doubt dependent on her. That explains a great deal to me, Miss Harcourt,' Detherfield told her.

His superior smile irritated Dorothea even while she found his face and figure attractively masculine and his deft handling of the reins as he drove very impressive. The man was arrogant and rude to assume so much about her. 'Nothing of the sort,' she retorted at once and sighed in relief as the hotel came into view. Then a thought entered her head and she realized how improper it would seem to be dropped at the door by a strange male. What if her aunt or any other

13

guests should see? Instead she said hurriedly, 'If you could please set me down in Matlock Bath near the cottages I will walk to my lodgings from there. I am grateful for the ride.'

He stifled a chuckle. He had seen her glance guiltily at the hotel and draw her shawl round her shoulders as if seeking to hide, but even as he slowed to a stop he heard her exclaim in horror beside him.

'Oh dear! Oh please sir, set me down quickly. I must get down.'

Her agitation was strange after the self-possessed way she had spoken to him and even accused him, and his glance at once took in a lovely young girl walking beside a thin, pimply youth who was holding her hand in open-mouthed adoration.

'I am delighted to have been of assistance, Miss Harcourt,' he said, jumping down and coming round to help her alight.

For a moment Dorothea forgot the sight of Clio with an unknown young man as she felt strong arms round her. She was lifted as if she had been a featherweight and set gently on her feet. His clasp had been pleasantly exciting but then thoughts of Clio came back to her. After thanking him again abruptly she rushed away across the road to wrest her cousin from trouble.

Detherfield set his horses in motion again and glanced back, to see Miss Harcourt drawing the beautiful blond girl away from the young man with every sign of annoyance. He chuckled aloud. She was a refreshing change from the spoiled beauties he normally escorted and had made an amusing interlude in the day, but he intended to dismiss her from his mind as the curricle moved on.

Dorothea was unable to dismiss Martin Detherfield easily from her thoughts, but for some minutes she was too absorbed with Clio and the persistent young man even to recall her own recent adventure.

'Clio, you must return to the hotel with me at once.' She reprimanded her young cousin as quietly as she could.

The familiar pout settled on Clio's lovely features and she relinquished her beau's hand with ill grace. 'I was enjoying a short walk, that's all Dorothea,' she muttered crossly. 'You have been out so why shouldn't I go too?'

'You should have taken Annie with you,' Dorothea objected, knowing that to say this was hypocrisy since she had been walking alone, but then she was five years older and far less susceptible than Clio. Or was she? Dismissing the dark-haired, dark-eyed gentleman from her thoughts with an effort she turned briskly to the pimply youth.

'I thank you for escorting my cousin, but we are returning to our hotel now. I bid you good day.'

He doffed his hat and nodded his head but fell into step beside them. 'I was so pleased to meet Miss Harcourt,' he said, breaking into eager speech. 'I was at the assembly last night and I could hardly take my eyes off her. You are so beautiful,' he said to Clio with admiration.

The romantic Clio took in such flattery with delight and simpered prettily, but Dorothea was annoyed with the young man, recognizing the impropriety of such a speech. Since her cousin had been wandering the street unattended it was not surprising she had been accosted. However, the fellow could not be allowed to continue with such pretensions.

'It was pleasant to have met you Mr . . . er . . . ?'

'Mr Simmonds, at your service,' he murmured, still walking beside them.

'Well, Mr Simmonds, no doubt we will see you again. Goodbye,' Dorothea said firmly.

Refusing to take the hint Mr Simmonds addressed himself to Clio. 'Oh, will you let me escort you for a promenade tomorrow, Miss Harcourt? I should be delighted to do so.'

Before Clio could reply Dorothea broke in ruthlessly. 'I am afraid that will not be possible. We are already engaged tomorrow. Now if you will excuse us we must hurry back to the hotel. Good day, Mr Simmonds.' Pulling Clio along beside her, Dorothea was glad to see Mr Simmonds stop and hesitate. He looked forlorn and very young but she refused to feel any sympathy. She knew that it was her cousin's foolishness in walking out alone that had caused the little incident and wondered how to broach this without betraying her own worse folly.

Clio was too good-natured to mind very much the way she had been detached from the young man. She walked happily beside Dorothea and turned her attention to her cousin.

'Why, you look very untidy, Dottie!' she exclaimed after a moment. 'What has been happening to you? I never saw you walking in the street, either. Where did you appear from?'

Wishing she had stopped at the hotel to tidy herself Dorothea sighed. She would have to tell the truth and then caution her cousin while admitting her own fault. 'I'm afraid I had a slight accident on the road. I nearly fell under a carriage. The gentleman was driving far too recklessly,' she added, remembering his familiarity and also the strength in his arms. 'However, he gave me a lift in his curricle back into Matlock, which is why I am somewhat dishevelled.'

'Oh dear, Dottie! Were you hurt?' Clio exclaimed in distress. She clasped her cousin by the arm and patted her hand. 'What a horrid experience. No wonder you are out of sorts and did not appreciate Mr Simmonds's attentions. He is so kind,' she added happily. 'And so admiring.'

'Maybe he is, but it was very improper of you to speak to him without an introduction,' Dorothea said quickly. 'I am sure he is quite harmless, but you should have had Annie with you at least. You must not wander round unescorted, for you are too young and innocent.'

'Well, Mr Simmonds was escorting me,' Clio replied, quite unruffled by the scold. 'And I did not see you with Annie either, Dottie. Should you not have taken her yourself?'

'Yes, I should have done. In fact we should all have gone out together,' Dorothea admitted with a sigh as they walked into the drive of the hotel. 'We were both wrong and must not be so foolish again. What would Aunt Sophie say?'

'You will not tell her?'

'No indeed. I would hate to upset her.'

'Oh good. Poor Mama needed her rest but I got bored sitting beside her so I thought I would take just a little walk. I do realize it was wrong not to take Annie, but she was nowhere to be seen. I will go with you in future, Dottie.'

'Good girl. Ah, at last we are back. I am quite windblown and untidy. I hope we will not see anyone we know before we reach our rooms,' Dorothea said as they entered the hotel.

She was destined to be disappointed in her wish. Mrs Howard was just going into the parlour as they walked through the door, but she turned back as she saw them and raised her eyebrows archly at Dorothea.

'Did I see you whirl past in a handsome curricle only a few moments ago, Miss Harcourt?' she asked.

'Yes indeed,' Dorothea said, furious that this particular guest should see her in such a state. 'If you will excuse us we must dress for dinner.'

'Oh yes, of course. But pray, will you grant me a few words first, Miss Harcourt?' Mrs Howard said.

Dorothea sighed. 'Go on up, Clio. I will join you in a moment,' she told the younger girl and obediently Clio disappeared up the stairs. 'Now what can I do for you, Mrs Howard?' she asked wearily.

'Oh do call me Samantha. Mrs Howard is so formal and so ageing, don't you think? I feel we are going to be friends. Now if you could just come into the parlour we can speak privately.'

Since Mrs Howard had taken her arm, Dorothea had little choice but to accompany the woman. Good manners prevented her from joining Clio upstairs but she wished heartily that the next few minutes were over.

'Now, dear Dorothea — that is your name is it not?' Mrs Howard said as she drew the girl down to sit on a chair beside her just inside the parlour door. 'I couldn't help noticing you riding in that carriage and although you went by so fast I recognized you. Was that not a teeny bit careless of you to be seen unchaperoned? Even with such a fine gentleman.' Her bright eyes regarded Dorothea with frank curiosity.

'I had an unfortunate accident on the road and was nearly run down. Mr Detherfield kindly gave me a lift back into Matlock Bath, that is all. It was nothing. There was hardly room for my maid in the vehicle,' she added, hoping Mrs Howard would think Annie had been with her.

'Oh no, naturally not,' Samantha Howard

murmured, ignoring this. 'Mr Detherfield you say? Now that is most amusing. Did he tell you that was his name?'

'Yes indeed he did.'

'Don't sound so stiff and outraged, my dear. These gentlemen will have their fun. Mr Detherfield, oh that's rich!' She broke into a peal of rather loud laughter and Dorothea's anger and resentment grew.

'What is his name then?' she asked because, in spite of her temper, she was very curious about her rescuer. 'Do you know him?'

'Oh, not exactly, my dear. I know of him, I suppose you would say. But Mr Detherfield — that is very amusing, indeed it is. However, I did not ask you in here to talk of gentlemen. In fact they were far from my thoughts. You know, you remind me so much of another lady I once knew, one I knew very well.'

'Possibly,' said Dorothea quietly. 'My looks are unremarkable though, ma'am, and I think could remind you of several ladies.'

'Oh, not several; just one. A very special one who carried a picture of a little girl and who moved so well in the capitals of Europe. Do you get my meaning?' she added delicately.

Dorothea felt her stomach churn instinctively. Surely this woman could not have

21

known her mama. It was impossible and yet it sounded horribly as if she had. There had to be a mistake, yet why did Dorothea remind her of someone?

'I don't know what you mean.' Dorothea rose from her chair.

'Oh yes, I think you do. I can understand you not wishing to tell anyone the truth. I doubt if I would in your place, my dear. Does your aunt, Mrs Harcourt, and little Clio know? Oh, I see they don't,' she added smugly as Dorothea started. 'Well, you would hate them to learn the truth, would you not?'

'Yes I would, for it could ruin Clio's chances of a good match,' Dorothea said bluntly. She was tired of this fencing. 'What do you want from me? Is it money? I cannot imagine anything else I could do for you.'

'Could you not? Well, I will tell you but not straight away. First I think, as I said, that we should become friends. I have a great desire to visit an assembly in Buxton tomorrow where a grand ball is being held. Why don't we go together? I can act as chaperon for you girls and so save your aunt the trouble.'

Dorothea was not quite sure whether she was hearing aright. This wretched woman seemed to be suggesting a social outing, no doubt paid for by Dorothea, but it was hard to imagine why. Had her fall hurt her head?

She thought not but this whole interview was so puzzling and upsetting. She rubbed her forehead absently. 'I don't know what my aunt would say. It is a long drive to Buxton and the roads are poor. We might not get back easily at night.'

'Oh yes we will, my dear. Leave all the arrangements to me. Little Clio will be so excited at the prospect, I'm sure. I will give you the details in the morning.' Without waiting for any more objections from the bewildered girl Mrs Howard swept out of the parlour. When Dorothea reached the doorway she had disappeared from sight.

Wondering what on earth she had let herself in for and why this dreadful woman wanted their company Dorothea slowly mounted the stairs to her chamber.

Her mama's secret was not as safe as she had hoped and as the lawyer had promised. If she refused to go would Mrs Howard tell everyone? It was a sad dilemma and she felt the beginnings of a headache as she worried over the problem.

2

As Mrs Howard had foreseen, Clio was enchanted at the prospect of attending an assembly in the neighbouring town of Buxton, at the far more famous assembly rooms there. She had been ecstatic when the idea was mentioned diffidently by Dorothea at dinner that night. Mrs Harcourt had been far more doubtful but when she was fully aware that there was no need for her to go herself then she regarded the plan more favourably.

'How can we afford it?' she whispered to Dorothea as the first covers were removed. The hotel dining room was half-full and she had no wish to be overheard.

'Oh, Mrs Howard is seeing to all the arrangements, Aunt Sophie,' Dorothea said quickly.

'How very kind of her,' Clio put in, clasping her hands together eagerly and smiling across the room at the lady in question. Mrs Howard responded majestically in kind and the plumes on her purple turban nodded almost into her ratafia cream. 'Why do you think she has asked us to accompany her? Are we not fortunate that she has singled us out?'

Privately Dorothea thought they were most

unlucky. She had no wish for Clio to be seen in the company of such a vulgar and encroaching female as Samantha Howard appeared to be. The woman called herself a widow and must be well over thirty summers, but although still handsome in a fair and florid way was already running to fat and her taste in clothes was too extreme to be pleasing. Her gown of emerald silk with a low décolletage was trimmed lavishly with purple ribbons to match the turban, and again she was wearing too much jewellery, although her diamonds looked real and of quality. How had such a woman known her mama? Surely they had not been friends? Even as that thought disgusted her Dorothea realized that now Samantha Howard knew her secret it mattered little how friendly she had been with her mother. The secret had to be kept and what was one evening's entertainment? She must hope that Mrs Howard would want to see no more of them afterwards.

'I believe she wanted some company, and most of the other guests here are elderly.' Dorothea answered Clio as quietly as she could. It would not do to let her cousin know how much she disliked Mrs Howard.

'Oh yes, that must be the reason. But what a treat for us, Dottie.' Clio was looking so pretty in her excitement that even the elderly and infirm gentlemen in the room were staring at her with pleasure and a few with envy. 'I did not think you liked Mrs Howard?' Clio added with one of her more perceptive stares at her cousin. 'Have you changed your mind? I am sure that I have now that she has asked us out.'

Wishing Clio had more discernment, Dorothea stifled a sigh. 'She has many good points I am sure, Clio, and is certainly kind to ask us to go out with her. I'm just concerned about Aunt Sophie,' she added to change the subject. 'Will you be happy here on your own?' she asked that lady quickly.

'You know I will, Dorothea,' her aunt said placidly. Now that she had accepted the idea of the outing she had little further interest in the plans. 'I will have my dinner sent up to my room and enjoy an early night. It is a pity we couldn't afford a private parlour here, but never mind. I will be quite happy. I have a new novel from the lending library which I brought from home and have not read yet.'

Reassured about her aunt but still troubled about the plan, Dorothea went to bed that night and slept little. She had not worried unduly about the secret confided to her by the lawyer concerning her mama. It had been something of a shock to learn that she had not been orphaned, just deserted, but she had no recollection of the woman who had given her birth, so she did not allow the fact to distress her.

The inheritance was very welcome, for the little family was in dire straits after her uncle's death and had all but used up what he had left. She had hated keeping her aunt in ignorance about the source of her money and had been glad when her tale of a distant relative leaving her a house and a small income had been readily accepted. The lawyer had been insistent that to lay claim to the whole sum publicly would cause just the comment he wished to avoid and which could be damaging to both Dorothea's and Clio's future happiness.

Now, as she tossed and turned in bed, Dorothea wished the kindly little man had said more and that she had not accepted the facts related to her so easily. If she was to encounter many other people with knowledge similar to that possessed by Mrs Howard she would never succeed in launching her lovely cousin successfully. It was a great worry.

She gained some reassurance next day when Mrs Howard informed her that it was to be a masked ball with unveiling at eleven as the assembly ended. This exciting news sent Clio and Annie running to the nearby shops to buy the necessary silk masks, while

Dorothea retired to her room to go through her wardrobe and select a dress to wear, thankful that at least they might be spared from acknowledging their companion for almost the entire evening. Nobody in Buxton was likely to know their family either, since they had journeyed to the spa from Bedfordshire where her uncle had a modest estate. In this year of 1810, people they met would probably accept them happily without asking too many questions.

Dorothea had very few dresses suitable for a large assembly. She pulled out one of pale-primrose silk and discarded it as being too simple. If they were to be in Mrs Howard's company she could hardly provide too great a contrast and the simplicity must be left for Clio. She chose her most elaborate gown of ivory tussore with an embroidered overskirt of a darker shade of cream and similar embroidery on the puff sleeves. The neckline was modest and the dress was caught below her breast with knots of ribbon. It had taken her many hours to make with Annie's help and she was very proud of her efforts but it was unlikely to be as fashionable as the gowns they would see in Buxton. Thankful that she had not persuaded Aunt Sophie to go to Bath after all, for that would have required even more gowns, Dorothea hurried in to help Clio with her *toilette*.

An early dinner in Mrs Howard's private parlour had been bespoken by that lady and the carriage was to collect them at five o'clock to convey them to Buxton. The journey would take an hour, for it was more than ten miles away. They sat down to eat chicken, lobster patties, galantine of hare and numerous sweet pastries and syllabubs and Dorothea allowed herself to look forward to the evening for the first time in twenty-four hours. Masked, nobody would know them and she loved dancing. She and Clio had only been taught in the schoolroom and had had little practice except at a few local assemblies and select gatherings in the private houses of friends in Bedfordshire.

Clio was too excited to eat much and Dorothea too nervous about the prospect ahead, for she knew she would have to keep watch over her volatile young cousin. Mrs Howard was certainly not going to Buxton to chaperon a young girl, but for motives of her own.

'Oh do hurry and finish the meal,' Clio begged, as Mrs Howard took yet another pastry. It was not surprising, Dorothea thought unkindly, that the woman was plump. 'I am so looking forward to this evening. Will there be many handsome gentlemen there?' she asked the older woman.

Mrs Howard wiped her hands and finished her glass of wine. 'I hope so, my dear. We are going for that, are we not? To see and be seen by handsome gentlemen.' She gave a chuckle and gazed at Dorothea. 'Perhaps Mr Detherfield might be there. Would you care to meet him again?' she enquired innocently.

Feeling herself blushing and furious at her own weakness when she remembered that dark, mocking face gazing down at her by the roadside and the strong arms that had held her so briefly, Dorothea sighed. 'I doubt if I would recognize him or he me, ma'am.'

'Oh do call me Samantha, dear. I am sure he will remember but we shall see.' She chuckled again and Dorothea wondered just who this Mr Detherfield was that Mrs Howard should find his name so amusing.

Clio also enquired about the mysterious gentleman as they climbed into the carriage and settled down for the drive. Dorothea explained this was the person who had nearly run her down, then given her a lift, but she discouraged further comment and Clio eventually fell silent, too overcome by excitement at the evening ahead to worry about her cousin's strange abruptness and unwillingness to discuss the gentleman.

All three ladies had grown tired of the jolting action of the carriage when at last

Buxton was reached. The discomfort of the journey was soon forgotten as they gazed at the lighted streets and the many inns and hotels. People strolled on pavements and a general air of festivity hung over the place. It was difficult to gain a good view of the famous crescent where the Grand Assembly room was situated but Clio craned her neck out of the carriage window and even Dorothea stared at the impressive buildings as the carriage joined the slowly moving throng of vehicles depositing other ladies and gentlemen at the doors.

Mrs Howard insisted that they don their masks on their way inside. She put her own on with great aplomb, the feathers in her headdress quivering impressively. For once even Dorothea was glad to be with her.

The assembly room itself was a large chamber as high as it was wide and decorated in blue and gilt in a most impressive manner. The dress balls being held on Wednesdays, which this was, were popular events. Ladies and gentlemen were already dancing on the floor. Side chambers led off to rooms for cards and billiards to amuse those not interested in the dancing and many chairs were provided for the chaperons. Dorothea was rather alarmed to see that few ladies were not escorted by gentlemen but she hid her qualms for Clio's sake.

Mrs Howard led the way to the chairs and seated herself, fanning her face so vigorously that her ostrich plumes waved as well. Dorothea was glad of the mask that hid part of her face for she saw at once that Mrs Howard was attracting the attention of several gentlemen and, from their ostentatious dress, appeared to be not the type she wished Clio to mix with. Yet now that they were in the assembly rooms there was little she could do but reply to Clio's excited comments and try to ignore her fears.

A young gentleman presented himself in front of them and bowed. 'May I have the honour of this dance?' he lisped sweetly to Clio, who dimpled up at him and accepted his proffered arm. He was the first of many who came to claim the girl's hand, which was a great relief to her cousin.

Dorothea also found she had no shortage of partners, but they were mostly older men to judge from their hair, dress and demeanour, even if their features were partly hidden by the masks. She enjoyed the dancing but knew she was surreptitiously looking for one particular man in the crowd and she chided herself for her folly. It was very unlikely that Martin Detherfield would attend this assembly and she was not even sure whether she would recognize him if he did so.

When at last a tall, dark-haired man walked across the room towards her she knew at once it was him. He wore a dark-blue evening coat so expertly tailored as to make him stand out even if his height had not already done so. His breeches were of black Florentine silk and black-silk stockings set off well-muscled calves. She drew in a deep breath of pleasure. Was he going to speak to her? Beside her Mrs Howard, at that moment without an attendant admirer, dug her in the ribs and that lady's coarse chuckle made Dorothea wince. It seemed that masks were not sufficient disguise, for Samantha at any rate.

Detherfield stopped in front of her and bowed. He held out a hand and smiled, making her heart thump erratically. 'May I have the pleasure of this dance?' he asked.

'Why, thank you, sir,' she said politely and accepted his hand as she got to her feet.

They walked over to the set that was forming for the quadrille. 'Have you been here long?' he asked as the music began. 'I have only just arrived, I'm afraid. My coach was held up outside Buxton.'

'Not by another lady tripping over her shawl I hope,' Dorothea said lightly, then could have bitten out her tongue. What on earth had made her make such a stupid remark? She had now given away her identity completely and also informed him that she recognized him too, which might not please him.

To her great relief he laughed. 'I am so glad you are not going to pretend not to recognize me, Miss Harcourt. I dislike coy and simpering misses.'

'Clumsy I may be but not coy, I hope.'

'Good. I came to this assembly in the hopes that you might attend. Are you with a large party?' he enquired as they progressed down the room.

Dorothea blushed and hoped he was not looking at her face. She did not wish to admit they had no gentleman escort. 'I came with my cousin and a chaperon,' she told him at last deciding to be honest.

'It is a long drive from Matlock Bath. Do you stay here for the night or return after the unmasking?'

'Oh, we must return. My aunt remains in the hotel and I would not care to worry her by staying here without her.'

'Who then is your chaperon?' he asked, intrigued by this fresh mystery.

Once again Dorothea was embarrassed and her reply was stilted. 'A lady staying at the hotel was good enough to act in that capacity.'

'Indeed. I collect you are not too happy about that?'

'Mr Detherfield, you ask a great many questions,' Dorothea said coolly. 'I fear our arrangements are not of such great interest as all that.'

'Oh but they are. I thought I recognized the lady sitting beside you when I approached you just now.'

'Do you know her, sir?' Fresh misgivings flooded through Dorothea and she missed her step in the dance.

Ignoring her lapse Mr Detherfield murmured, 'I know her type, is perhaps a better explanation. Not the most suitable chaperon, if I might advise, for such a young lady as yourself.' Dorothea was well aware of this and to have Mr Detherfield point it out only increased her embarrassment. In her dismay she gave an impatient exclamation.

'Sir! I would prefer not to discuss the matter if you please.' Then, remembering Mrs Howard's own comments on Mr Detherfield, she could not refrain from adding, 'Our chaperon has also heard of you, sir, but not under the name you gave me.'

The man at her side stiffened at once and she felt his fingers grip her own tightly for a moment before they relaxed. 'Oh really,' he drawled. 'Maybe it is a case of mistaken identity. I should surely know my own name, Miss Harcourt.'

'Yes I know,' she agreed ruefully. 'I think she must have made a mistake if you say so. I am sorry to have mentioned it but I was surprised.'

'Martin Detherfield is certainly my name,' he said quietly. 'Did she perhaps say who she thought I was?' Once again his clasp increased slightly.

Unnerved and excited by the contact Dorothea was thrown off balance and was not quite her usual calm self. 'No indeed. She merely laughed.'

'I see. Well I shouldn't worry your pretty head about it, then,' he said cheerfully and Dorothea had the strangest feeling that he was pleased about something.

'Now let us talk instead of the beauties of the area. I hope you intend to visit one or two of the large houses in the vicinity during your stay. Chatsworth is truly magnificent but perhaps a little far from Matlock for your aunt to travel. However, Rothley Hall is much nearer and I am sure you would enjoy a day spent there. The grounds include a series of small lakes.'

'It sounds delightful but does the owner permit visitors?' Dorothea asked. She was glad of the change of subject.

'I believe so but I am not sure. Now,' he said as the dance ended and he led her from the floor, 'if you are not engaged for the next set may I offer you some lemonade?'

'I should enjoy that. Thank you.' Dorothea sat down and watched him stride away to procure the drink. His shoulders were so broad that the cloth of his coat rippled, showing his muscles, and she sighed. He was still a complete stranger to her but she believed him when he said his name was Detherfield. Mrs Howard must have been confusing him with somebody else. She was glad to see that their so-called chaperon was engaged in dancing with a very plump man in satin knee-breeches that looked in danger of splitting as he twirled her around. Dorothea hid a smile behind her fan just as Mr Detherfield returned.

'They are amusing, are they not?' he murmured with a wicked grin as he followed her eyes. 'These assemblies produce some strange characters at times. But what is amiss?' he added, for her expression had changed to one of consternation.

'Oh, it is nothing,' Dorothea exclaimed, getting to her feet and nearly falling in her haste. He steadied her with an arm and placed her drink upon a small table.

'Tell me,' he commanded. 'I can see you

are upset. What is it?'

'My cousin. She has just left the room with a young man and I fear may do something foolish. I must find her.'

'We will both find her,' he said and took her arm to lead her around the floor. 'I imagine we are talking of the enchanting young girl with the blond curls dressed in white with blue ribbons,' he added. 'I also noticed her leave, but she cannot have gone far.'

'Her head is filled with so many silly romantic notions,' Dorothea apologized. 'She is so young, you see.'

'And you, of course, have already reached the age of discretion.'

'I am two and twenty, sir, so no longer a girl,' Dorothea explained. 'Do you think they have gone outside?'

'More likely into one of the small withdrawing rooms,' Mr Detherfield said, and led her through the door into another chamber. At the far end was a small room, its doorway partly hidden by a large potted fern. 'We may find them in here.'

Dorothea was so anxious about Clio she had forgotten she was still clutching Mr Detherfield's arm until he patted her hand reassuringly and pointed through the open doorway. 'There is your truant, I believe.'

Dorothea broke away from him and moved quickly towards Clio, who was trying to disengage herself from the inexpert embrace of an ardent young man. But Detherfield was before her. He yanked the youth away with scant disregard for his neckcloth and the young man's mask fell to the floor.

'Oh Dottie, I'm so sorry,' Clio wailed. 'He started to clutch me.'

Dorothea put an arm round her soothingly. 'Clio, you must never wander off at an assembly. You know what your mama would say. Poor Aunt Sophie.'

'I think we arrived in time,' Detherfield said quietly. 'Now be off, you silly young pup, and don't let me catch you ill-treating a lady again.'

The pimply, perspiring face of Mr Simmonds had been revealed when the mask fell off and Dorothea was not surprised. Clio had probably seen him that morning in Matlock and told him of their adventure, and he had decided to travel to Buxton as well. She was almost sorry for him as he cringed away from Mr Detherfield and slunk to the door.

'I . . . I must apologize, ladies. Got carried away,' he stuttered. 'You are so beautiful,' he cried to Clio, whose tears stopped immediately to be replaced by a radiant smile.

Detherfield's lips twitched and Dorothea

was hard put not to giggle. The scene was so ludicrous. The young man stumbled off and she turned to thank Detherfield for assisting in the rescue.

'Let me escort you both back to the dance floor where we may find your chaperon,' he murmured with a slight bow.

They had just reached the assembly room again and had paused in the doorway to look for Mrs Howard when another gentleman approached and clapped Detherfield on the shoulder.

'Martin! By all that's wonderful! What in God's name are you doing in a place like this? I could hardly believe the story when I heard it. When did you last attend a provincial assembly, old chap? Why, it must be soon after you were breeched.'

'Now now, James. Don't give away any secrets,' Detherfield said cheerfully but with a warning glance at the ladies. 'Let me introduce you to the Misses Harcourt. I am afraid I do not know their first names. This is James Sowerby,' he added.

With a puzzled glance at Martin Detherfield, James Sowerby bowed to the ladies. As he studied Clio's face and figure his eyes grew round with admiration. 'I am delighted to make your acquaintance. Now I can see why you are attending, Detherfield. Not surprised at all. May I have the pleasure?' he added gallantly, extending a hand to Clio as the music for the country dances began.

With her pretty little smile Clio gracefully accepted his proffered arm and was led on to the floor. Dorothea was grateful that her cousin's mind had so quickly been taken off the past few minutes and she relaxed slightly. Mrs Howard was not in sight but Mr Detherfield led her to the chairs they had vacated so speedily not long before.

'Please, don't let me keep you from your partners,' Dorothea told him, sinking on to a chair. 'I am most grateful for your intervention just now. I am afraid the young gentleman is staying in Matlock, as we are, and has become infatuated with Clio.'

'What a charming name your cousin has,' Detherfield mused as he took the seat beside her. 'Yes, I thought I recognized the young puppy as the one who was with her yesterday when you left my curricle so precipitately.'

'I hoped you had not noticed.' Dorothea blushed again and cursed this weakness that betrayed her agitation.

'Are you responsible for your young relative?' he enquired easily. 'She is a delightful little thing, but perhaps unworldly as yet.'

'Oh yes, she has no experience at all but I

hope she will make her come-out next season,' Dorothea explained quickly, glad to find he was so understanding. 'She has a charming nature but she is also very innocent and very susceptible,' she murmured ruefully.

'So we saw just now. You, I imagine, are not likely to allow a handsome face or figure to sway you so easily.'

'Certainly not, sir,' Dorothea told him coolly. She was not sure whether he was teasing her or not, as his expression gave nothing away.

'I believe I heard your cousin call you Dottie. An unusual name if I may say so, Miss Harcourt.' Now she was sure his lips were twitching with amusement and she was annoyed at his presumption. She knew nothing about him, after all, yet he was quizzing her as if she were a lady of the town.

'A family pet name, sir, that is all. And since you are a stranger to me I believe my name is not your business.'

Totally ignoring her snub he mused on. 'Now Dottie could be short for Dorothy, or for Donna perhaps, or even Dora.'

'Sir,' Dorothea exclaimed, torn between outrage and amusement. In the end amusement won and she giggled, even though this was a most improper conversation.

'I see I shall have to tell you or you will be

thinking me totally brainless. Your first guess was the nearest, for my name is Dorothea.'

His dark eyes sparkled with satisfaction. 'I am glad you decided not to be offended, Miss Harcourt. I wished to know your name and as we have no chaperon present to introduce us properly it was naturally left to me to take the honour upon myself.'

'Oh, naturally.'

'And your family?' he enquired. 'Do they also stay in Matlock with your aunt and cousin too?'

Dorothea shook her head and sighed. She had no wish to speak of her family at all and she noticed Mrs Howard approaching. It was not a subject to be discussed in front of that woman. 'My parents are both dead,' she said hurriedly. 'I live with my aunt and cousin now.'

'I am sorry,' he said, sounding sincere. He got to his feet as he, too, saw Mrs Howard. 'I thank you for the dance and the lively conversation, Miss Harcourt. Your servant.' He swept her a courtly bow and walked off just as Mrs Howard plumped down in the seat he had vacated.

'What a pity he has gone,' the older woman panted. 'I had hoped to speak to him and to be introduced.'

'But I thought you knew him?'

43

'Oh, I told you I knew of him,' Mrs Howard remarked airily, waving her hands in the air. The diamonds on her thick fingers caught the light from the candles behind them and gleamed brightly, creating glittering sausages. 'He stands out in a crowd like this so we could not fail to recognize him. I wonder if he will come over to you again?'

'I doubt it,' said Dorothea dismissively. She had no wish to encourage Mrs Howard in idle speculation but she secretly hoped he would ask her for another dance. The whole evening had been worth while after all, with one dance and the interlude with him. They had conversed more like old friends than strangers but she did not care. Mrs Howard chatted on and remarked on the graceful dancing and trim figure of the gentleman with Clio.

'Who is he?' she asked, tapping her fan on her wrist. 'I do not know him, I think, but maybe when he unmasks later on I shall remember his face.'

'James Sowerby, so he said,' Dorothea told her. 'Have you met him?'

'I think not. The name has a familiar ring to it, yet I cannot recall just who he is. Clio certainly seems enchanted by him as a partner at all events.'

Dorothea had to agree that her cousin did

look very happy. The mask could not hide her beauty and the couple drew all eyes as they danced around the floor.

When the music ceased James Sowerby returned her to them and bowed before striding off.

'Who is he?' Mrs Howard asked at once.

'Mr Sowerby? Oh a perfect gentleman,' Clio breathed. 'He is just as I imagine my hero will be. Do you think he is handsome under the mask? I am so looking forward to eleven when I shall be able to see him.'

'Perhaps he will not stay that long,' Dorothea suggested prosaically.

Clio looked horrified but quickly accepted the hand of another young gentleman bowing before her and skipped away. She whirled into the next dance and seemed just as happy as she had been before.

Both girls were destined to be disappointed in their hopes. However hard she looked among the throng, Dorothea could no longer see the upright figure of Mr Detherfield and she wondered if he had retired to play cards. Supper came and they were escorted by three elderly gentlemen who had been waiting to pounce on them. Only Mrs Howard was happy but Clio had too many eager gentlemen around her to feel bored for long. Yet when the assembly drew to a close promptly at eleven of the

45

clock neither Mr Detherfield nor Mr Sowerby were amongst those unmasking and both girls were quiet on the long journey back in the coach. Only Mrs Howard chatted brightly on all they had seen and done until Dorothea feigned sleep to keep from making unnecessary replies.

3

Next morning both girls slept very late. It was after eleven o'clock when Dorothea awoke to find Annie pulling the curtains back from the windows.

'Are you ready for your chocolate, miss?' the maid said hopefully. 'I thought I heard you stir so I came in. Did you enjoy the assembly? Was it very exciting?'

Dorothea smiled at Annie's eager expression. The maid had cared for all three ladies for five years and although still young played the part of an old retainer and entered into whatever they did. Clio's excitement at the prospect of the assembly at Buxton had transmitted itself to Annie and now she wanted to hear all about it. Dorothea described some of the company and how popular her cousin had been.

'There is no doubt that Clio was the belle of the assembly even though we all wore masks. She was surrounded by admirers all evening. I do hope the attention has not gone to her head. Is she awake yet?' she asked as she sipped her chocolate and nibbled at a roll.

Annie shook her head. 'I popped my head

in to see but she was lying like a little angel and still dreaming of some fine gentleman from the smile around her mouth. Miss Clio is a real romantic.'

Dorothea was aware of this and the problems involved as a result but she wisely chose not to comment, glad that her young cousin had enjoyed such a marvellous evening. Her own had been mixed. She was still very doubtful of the propriety of their trip and Mrs Howard was certainly no proper chaperon, as Mr Detherfield had pointed out to her embarrassment. Maybe it was because of this that he had not come to claim her for another dance. She sighed and wished she had never gone out walking alone and so recklessly fallen near his carriage. He was just the type of gentleman to disturb her peace of mind and she had thought never to meet one like him. However, dreaming would not do for her and she quickly got out of bed. There was no chance she would meet the man again as they were only to be in Matlock Bath a little longer. It would be better to put him out of her mind altogether and prepare to enjoy their last few days in the area.

This resolve was firmly in her mind as she attended on her Aunt Sophie. She was pleased to find that her relative had enjoyed a good dinner and an excellent night's rest.

Once again Dorothea had to describe the events of the previous evening and when Clio joined them they all discussed the assembly thoroughly until Mrs Harcourt was satisfied she had heard all the details.

'I almost feel I was there myself, you have described the scene so vividly,' she declared as they left her room and walked down the stairs to the hotel parlour. 'I am so glad you both had the opportunity to visit Buxton and I must thank Mrs Howard for so kindly organizing the trip and chaperoning you. Without her you would have been unable to attend.'

Dorothea thought privately that that might well have been a good thing, as she trailed in her aunt's wake carrying her shawl and her embroidery. She settled her aunt in a comfortable chair and gave her the sewing. It had not escaped Dorothea's notice that Clio had been particularly enraptured in her descriptions of James Sowerby; she clearly remembered him above all her other admirers.

It was a relief to know that Mr Simmonds was forgotten, but the chance of seeing Mr Sowerby again was remote. With a sigh Dorothea sat down beside the other two and listened as they went through the evening yet again.

Several days passed pleasantly enough with

walks, short trips to the nearby shops, which were not very impressive, and for Mrs Harcourt the important daily partaking of the waters. She declared each morning after she had consumed the liquid that she could feel the curative properties strengthening her and improving her health. Mrs Howard chatted to them occasionally but after preening herself on the success of the Buxton expedition she left the trio alone, to Dorothea's relief.

Two days before their departure for Bedfordshire Mrs Howard caught the girls in the entrance hall of the hotel. With a sweet smile that did not reach her eyes she declared that she had formed another plan for their entertainment. 'I thought you might like another carriage ride combined with a day's excursion before you return home,' she gushed.

'You are most kind but we cannot presume — ' Dorothea began.

'Oh, not at all, my dear,' Mrs Howard interrupted her. 'I have already organized the little trip because your sweet cousin thought it such a good idea when I mentioned it yesterday. We will set off tomorrow morning and view the scenery on our way to one of the beautiful mansions that grace this part of the world.'

'Chatsworth perhaps?' Dorothea suggested.

Samantha Howard's face fell at the name. 'Well, no, my dear. Too far away, although of course so very distinguished. I have settled on a house nearer than that since I thought your aunt would not want to be too fatigued by a long ride just before your journey home. I chose Rothley Hall, which is said to be very fine, if smaller than Chatsworth, and with lovely gardens and a series of lakes in the making.'

Remembering where she had heard the name before, Dorothea brightened slightly. Rothley Hall had been suggested by Mr Detherfield, so it must be a fine building for she trusted his good taste instinctively. Also the knowledge that Mrs Howard intended to include her aunt in the proposed expedition relieved her mind somewhat. Aunt Sophie might be vague and slightly muddled at times but she would prove a better chaperon for Clio if any young men were encountered.

'Of course, I have made the arrangements as before. You remember our little agreement?' Mrs Howard added meaningfully.

Dorothea nodded her head wearily. She had paid for the entire Buxton trip and would now be expected to do the same for Rothley Hall. She had no objection to doing so for the pleasure of her aunt and cousin but knowing that Samantha Howard had forced her to do so by use of blackmail made the affair distasteful from the start.

However Clio was delighted with the scheme and even Mrs Harcourt roused herself to show enthusiasm. Clio spent most of the day deciding which of her dresses was the most becoming and chose a pale-blue muslin with a high waist gathered under the bust with tiny knots of brighter blue ribbon, while similar ribbon knots decorated the puffed sleeves. Her chip-straw bonnet was very fetching and was also decorated with similar ribbons. Dorothea had helped in the making of this gown and her own more modest primrose muslin. This was plainer and trimmed with just a little lace, yet it suited her brown hair and provided a perfect foil for Clio's beauty.

Mrs Harcourt remarked on how pretty the girls looked as they set out in the open carriage the next day. 'We older ladies must admit they do us credit,' she said placidly, not noticing the frown on Samantha Howard's face at being so described. The widow was again overdressed in lavender silks with a matching silk bonnet and an amethyst ring on her finger with a necklace of the same stones.

It was such a beautiful day that Dorothea forgot her qualms about being once again in Mrs Howard's company and began to enjoy herself. The scenery was truly beautiful, larks sang in the sky and in no time it seemed they were bowling through ornate wrought-iron gates and down a long winding drive through pleasant parkland. When the mansion came into view it was seen to be not too large but of very fine proportions. It was built of mellowed red Tudor bricks, with fine chimneys standing up at each end of the imposing front. Their carriage stopped in the stable yard and when they had alighted Mrs Howard led the way into the house itself. The housekeeper was there to show them round and they all marvelled at the staircase sweeping up from the great central hall, the fine panelling in the library and the exquisite taste in the furniture, paintings and ornaments on display.

Dorothea was more comfortable once they had left the building and were able to wander through the grounds. It was too disconcerting to gape at somebody's home and she was afraid the owner might come upon them suddenly. The housekeeper had reassured them that the Earl of Rothley, who owned the hall, was a fine gentleman and not at all high in the instep, but she had not wanted to meet him.

Clio shared her feelings, it seemed. The two girls wandered away from the older ladies, who were suffering from the heat and who chose to sit awhile on chairs placed beside an ornamental garden.

'I was terrified the earl would suddenly appear and order us all to leave,' Clio said, giggling as they walked along.

'I am surprised he allows visitors when he is in residence,' Dorothea admitted. 'Still, I expect he is paying a call himself, or is shut into private apartments that we did not see.'

'Well, I hope he stays there until after we leave,' Clio cried and skipped a few steps. 'Oh, I do wish we could stay in Matlock a little longer, Dottie. I don't want to return home tomorrow, do you?'

'No. But then I hope I can persuade Aunt Sophie to let us go to London later on and take a lease on a house for the season. If she will permit it there will be plenty to look forward to.'

Clio clasped her hands together and stood quite still. 'Oh, do you think she will let us?' she breathed. 'Oh, I would like that above all things. We might even see James Sowerby again for such a fashionable gentleman would surely be in London for the season.'

'Did he say so?' Dorothea enquired with interest. Her own heartbeat increased at the notion, for if Mr Sowerby was in London then perhaps Mr Detherfield might be too, as they were friends.

Clio nodded and her curls danced under her bonnet.

'Yes indeed. He said he never came to such assemblies as the one we attended but he had heard that this friend was coming and he wanted to know the reason why. Strange, was it not?'

'Do you suppose his friend was that Mr Detherfield, who rescued me from Thomas?'

'Thomas?'

Clio gasped. 'Oh, Mr Simmonds I mean. You know, the pimply young man who behaved so badly. He really frightened me, Dottie,' she added as they strolled on.

'I expect Mr Sowerby had other friends at the assembly,' Dorothea murmured.

'He seemed surprised to see Mr Detherfield, after all.'

'So he did. Oh Dottie, do you hear voices?' They stopped and looked at each other in dismay as two men could be heard conversing on the other side of a nearby hedge.

'Perhaps they are visiting too?' Dorothea whispered.

'Let us go back to Mama,' Clio suggested softly and began to edge away.

They were too late. Around the corner of the hedge came two men deep in talk. When they realized that they were not alone they looked up and paused in amazement.

'Well, this is a pleasant surprise.' Martin Detherfield was the first to recover from the shock. 'I did suggest that you should visit Rothley Hall, and I see you have taken my advice,' he added to Dorothea.

James Sowerby gave his friend a keen glance, then bowed and lifted Clio's hand to his lips. 'This is my lucky day. I am glad I rode over to Rothley this morning. I had no idea I would meet the beauty again.' He bowed to Dorothea also but kept hold of Clio's hand.

Dorothea herself was too bemused at meeting in person the man she had been thinking about for the past half-hour, but as she recovered her wits she wondered what he was doing in the place.

'Are you visiting also, Mr Detherfield?' she enquired.

'Oh no, Martin is hardly a visitor!' James Sowerby exclaimed with a laugh. 'He is — '

'I am working here, yes I know, James, but allow me to tell the ladies myself.'

'Oh do you work here, Mr Detherfield? How interesting. And in such lovely surroundings too,' Dorothea exclaimed in her turn. She had noticed Mr Sowerby's expression of comical dismay and was curious about what he was going to say when his friend cut him short. 'What do you do?' she asked.

'Well, I suppose I shall have to admit it, but like most gentlemen I hate to own to doing a job of work,' Detherfield said ruefully.

'There is nothing to be ashamed of in honest labour,' Dorothea told him roundly. 'That is an excuse put about by those too lazy to do more than indulge themselves.'

'Oh quite, quite,' James Sowerby agreed hastily, casting a glance of desperation at his friend. He took Clio's hand in his and led her off but Mr Detherfield studied Dorothea in some surprise.

'You don't approve of idle gentlemen, then?' he enquired with interest.

'Not those who spend their time in gambling and frivolity alone, no, I don't think I do,' Dorothea admitted. 'You see, sir, I have not really been exposed to many such rich gentlemen, I am glad to say, so I have not thought about it often.'

'Good. Then you will not object to taking a walk with me and admiring my efforts,' he said cheerfully and tucked her arm into his.

They began to stroll in the opposite direction to that taken by Sowerby and Clio and once again Dorothea realized that this man was leading her into impropriety. 'My aunt and Mrs Howard are not far away,' she began. 'Should we not join them?'

'In a moment. First you must see what I

have been doing for the past three weeks.' They walked round the hedge and before them lay a small lake fed by a waterfall from another, set higher up. Beyond them there was yet another stretch of water with a vista opening out of trees and shrubs.

'It's beautiful,' Dorothea said in admiration. 'Did you do this?'

'Well, not the actual digging,' he said, hiding his amusement. 'I designed the lakes and the miniature cascade over here. Landscape gardening is my passion, although I cannot lay claim to the grandeur and magnificence of Capability Brown, for example.'

'This looks very fine to me,' Dorothea told him. 'You designed the whole yourself?'

'I did indeed. I'm glad you like it. Few people have seen what I've done and of course, it is not finished.'

'I suppose the trees and shrubs must take years to grow to full beauty but I can imagine how well it will look in the future,' she said thoughtfully, as she studied the view. 'Did the earl commission you to do this for him? If so you must be very good. Is he a friend of yours?'

Detherfield shrugged casually. 'I've known the earl all my life,' he replied. 'I am not a particularly brilliant designer yet, though. Have you seen any of Capability Brown's works? I especially like the park and vista he created at Petworth in Sussex. Do you know it at all?'

'I'm afraid not, sir. I have travelled little. However beautiful the gardens are that you refer to I am sure these are just as fine.'

'You are very kind. From your comments it is clear you have not yet visited Chatsworth.'

'We return home tomorrow, sir, and have no time to see more,' Dorothea said a little wistfully.

'Well, I am very glad that you made Rothley Hall your last visit, then,' Detherfield told her as he led her along the lakeshore. 'Now, before I return you to your aunt, give me the benefit of your advice.'

'I cannot advise you,' Dorothea told him, laughing up at him. 'I have no knowledge of gardens nor of landscaping. I just like what I see.'

'That is the most important thing,' he said seriously. 'I could plan innumerable vistas but unless those visitors who see them appreciate them I have wasted my time.'

'And the earl's money,' Dorothea put in.

He gave her a keen look which she met unflinchingly but she could not read the expression in his dark eyes. 'Very true,' he admitted at last. 'I must not waste the earl's money. So it is even more important for you to advise me. I have been wondering whether or not to erect a summerhouse where the middle lake drops into the bottom one. What do you think? Do you feel a Grecian temple would be appropriate? Or perhaps a simple affair would suit the surroundings. Tell me.'

Studying the area that he pointed out Dorothea considered for a moment. 'Not a temple, sir. I do admire the classical but I think it would be out of place in this rustic scenery. Perhaps a simple stone building, but I admit I prefer the view as it is. A summerhouse would intrude too much.'

'Maybe you are right,' he murmured. 'Yes, in fact I'm sure you are. Very well, Miss Harcourt, there will be no summerhouse.'

'But don't you have to consult your employer?' she queried.

'My employer? Oh I see. Of course. Well, the earl has given me a completely free hand to do as I wish. He will approve whatever I decide.'

'He must trust you then, Mr Detherfield, and have great faith in your abilities.'

'Oh yes. He certainly trusts me,' Detherfield murmured in a sardonic tone and she noticed a slight smile on his full lips. 'Still, enough of gardening and my pursuits. Have you enjoyed your stay in Matlock Bath?'

'Very much, sir. My aunt's health has

improved with daily partaking of the waters and it has been a pleasant change for us all.'

'Have you been bothered again by the young man who caused you so much trouble at the Buxton assembly?' he enquired with a lift of one dark eyebrow.

'Mr Simmonds has already left the area I'm glad to say,' Dorothea explained, rather reluctantly. She had no wish to remember that embarrassing scene, yet it was impossible not to think of the young man without giggling. He had been just like a puppy caught stealing a morsel of food. 'I think you frightened him, you see,' she added mischievously and they both laughed.

'I hope I did. Silly young fool. Anyway I'm pleased he has left your cousin alone.'

'Oh dear.' Dorothea stopped walking and looked around. They were still quite alone by the lake with the hedge on the other side. 'Where is Clio? She and Mr Sowerby have disappeared. Have they returned to my aunt?'

'I expect so,' he said cheerfully. 'She is safe enough with James, I assure you, so compose yourself, Miss Harcourt.'

'I, too, should go back to my aunt,' Dorothea added. She had no real wish to end this delightful conversation but she had been gone for a long while and her aunt might worry.

'I suppose you should,' he agreed. 'Very well then, let us go back. If we turn down here we can approach by another path and you can see the rest of the garden.'

They wandered along away from the lake chatting about many subjects. Dorothea was enjoying herself so much that she was sorry when they emerged at one end of the ornamental garden and could see the seat where her aunt and Mrs Howard were still sitting beneath a large tree.

'There they are,' Mr Detherfield said cheerfully. 'From their positions I suspect both ladies have been taking a short nap, so you will not have been missed. Now I must leave you and return to my tasks.'

'Thank you for showing me the lakes and the gardens. I have enjoyed my walk.'

'So have I,' he told her, giving her a slight bow. 'I hope I may have the pleasure of seeing you in London shortly. Did you not say you were hoping to be there for the Little Season?'

'Yes indeed.' Dorothea was now determined to persuade her aunt to agree to the proposed scheme if Mr Detherfield were to be in town. 'We shall be there.'

'Then we shall meet again soon. Your servant.' He gave her another bow and turned to walk away. Within a moment he had rounded another hedge and disappeared.

Dorothea went slowly back to the seat where Mrs Howard was now awake and had seen Mr Detherfield disappearing. 'Who was that?' she asked sharply, jolting the girl out of her pleasant dream.

'Oh, I met a gardener and he brought me back to this seat, for I lost my way,' she blurted out, not wanting Mrs Howard to start making sly innuendoes about Mr Detherfield.

'He was too well-dressed for a gardener,' Mrs Howard snorted. 'Are you sure he wasn't another visitor?'

'No, indeed. He was not an ordinary gardener but a landscape designer who has been creating a series of lakes beyond the formal garden,' Dorothea explained, hoping Mrs Howard would not ask any more awkward questions.

However, that lady had no interest in horticulture and she dismissed the man upon hearing this and began to unpack the basket they had brought with them. Dorothea was about to help lay out the simple picnic when Clio and Mr Sowerby appeared from behind them and Aunt Sophie woke up.

'Oh Dorothea, Clio, there you are. Have you had a nice walk?' Mrs Harcourt began sleepily.

'Who is this?' Mrs Howard said, addressing Clio but studying the young man who was bowing to them all.

'My name is James Sowerby,' he said quickly before Clio could reply. 'I rode over to Rothley this morning and was fortunate enough to meet your charming daughter in the gardens.' Mrs Howard bristled at being addressed as the mother of Clio. She considered herself too young for such a role but Mrs Harcourt was now fully awake and watching them all.

'This is my mama,' Clio told him, introducing her mother. James Sowerby apologized. He was so charming and his manners so good that the two older ladies were soon smiling happily and had forgiven him his mistake.

'Now, if you will excuse me I must go!' he told them sorrowfully after a few moments' conversation. 'I have to see the earl on several matters and I cannot keep him waiting.'

'No, of course not. We quite understand,' Mrs Howard gushed promptly. The mention of the earl had revived her. 'He is in residence, then? We rather thought so and hoped we might perhaps see him as we walked round.'

James Sowerby looked rather embarrassed at this. 'He is probably engaged on estate business,' he said, rather too quickly. He bowed again to them all, pressed Clio's hand

64

and walked off before Mrs Howard could ask any more awkward questions.

'What a charming young man. Is that the gentleman you met at the assembly the other night?' Mrs Harcourt asked her daughter. 'I can quite see why you found him so attractive. Such manners and such address,' she murmured hopefully. 'Do you know anything about him?' she enquired of Mrs Howard. 'Do you think he might have property in the area if he has business with the earl?'

'He could have.' Mrs Howard nodded. 'I am sure I have heard his name but, as I told the girls on Wednesday at the assembly, I do not recall any details. A pity, but no doubt I will remember in time. Now let us have something to eat for I am quite peckish with all this fresh air and walking.'

Mrs Howard had spent most of the outing sleeping on the seat and Dorothea hid a smile as she and Clio helped the older ladies to refreshment. It was a lovely sunny day and the grass was dry enough for them to spread their skirts and sit down. When they had finished the simple meal of cold chicken, rolls, small meat pies and fruit with some white wine and taken another turn in the grounds they were all ready to return to their hotel.

If Dorothea was disappointed that she did not see Mr Detherfield again she concealed her sentiments. Mrs Howard would have no further reason to tease and torment her if she could help it but she did wonder whether he had gone back to the lakes to further his schemes.

On the journey back to Matlock Mrs Howard monopolized the conversation.

'I do so hope that I will see you charming ladies again. I, too, am returning home shortly and I do not live too far away from you, for my little estate is in Buckinghamshire.'

'We would be delighted to see you, Mrs Howard, for you have been so kind to the girls,' Mrs Harcourt said kindly. 'You must visit us, but I warn you we live a very quiet life. Our house and estates are very modest now and our lives retiring since the death of my poor husband three years ago.' Dorothea helped to open her aunt's reticule to find her wispy handkerchief for the ritual dabbing of her eyes at mention of the deceased. Mrs Howard made clucking noises but she shot a triumphant glance at Dorothea, who ignored her.

'I should be delighted to visit. I also live in modest circumstances now, since I was widowed, but we can be a comfort to each other. You are so kind to invite me to stay. I shall look forward to a visit in the near future.' Emerging from her handkerchief Mrs Harcourt looked rather surprised at the speed with which her invitation had been taken up. She had only been mouthing the usual polite nothings and had not expected Mrs Howard to accept so readily.

'We live very quietly indeed,' she murmured in a slightly more anxious tone. 'We very seldom go out or even entertain now. I am sure you would find our little place too dull for you.' This was as far as she could go in attempting to put off the unwelcome guest for, although she had been grateful to what she thought was Mrs Howard's generosity in escorting her girls to Buxton and taking them all on this expedition, she could not really like the rather vulgar widow.

However Mrs Howard totally ignored this slight snub and instead elaborated on her plans. 'You live in Bedfordshire, do you not? A delightful county, as I know. Just outside Luton I think you said, Clio, did you not?'

'Yes indeed,' the young girl replied absently. 'Harcourt Manor it is called.' She relapsed into silence and from her expression was clearly still dreaming of her walk with James Sowerby.

Dorothea intervened. 'We will write to you when we are settled once more after this holiday and send you an invitation,' she said quickly. Once they were back home they could conveniently forget all about this dreadful woman. 'If you will give me your direction I will see to it for my aunt. There will be so much to do when we first get back after our holiday here as you must understand. I will let you know when it is convenient for a visit.'

Even Mrs Howard could not totally ignore this snub but the look she gave Dorothea made the girl quake inwardly. She was afraid of the threats and knew the damage exposure of her mother's secret could bring to Clio and her poor aunt, let alone her own future, but it would not do to let the woman know this. She smiled sweetly and saw her aunt look grateful for such a respite. Somehow, whatever the encroaching Mrs Howard attempted, Dorothea had to prevent her from visiting them and upsetting the family even if it did cost her money to do so.

Before they left Matlock Bath the next morning Mrs Howard managed to corner Dorothea alone. At once the girl knew her worst fears were to be realized.

'You will see I get an invitation to your aunt's house, I hope,' Samantha Howard said silkily but with a nasty look in her eye. 'I think you take my meaning, dear.'

'Why do you want to visit us?' Dorothea demanded. 'I cannot think why you insist on coming to stay. Our life is quiet and retired, as my aunt said.'

'Oh, I know that, but I may be able to liven you up a little,' the widow responded quickly.

'I am not sure when it will be convenient. My aunt's health is not good,' Dorothea said desperately.

'Possibly it is not, but I hope you will see to it that I do get invited and within the next two months. Otherwise, who knows where I shall spread your mama's secret? She was my best friend, you know. Think about what I've said, Dorothea. A short visit will not hurt, after all.' Dorothea nodded her head and pretended to agree. She had little choice and anyway could not prolong the conversation as her aunt was ready to leave.

They took their farewells of Mrs Howard with assurances of mutual esteem but she was determined to resist the widow's blackmail. Throughout the journey home she struggled with the problem and wondered how she could stall Mrs Howard and find a way of gaining Clio her season and seeing her well settled before the secret was exposed. Once Clio was married Mrs Howard could tell anyone she wished, for it would matter very little, or at least less. She had to be honest with herself for she knew exposure of the tale would ruin all her own chances of a future, but that was of minor importance. Somehow she must find a way to keep Mrs Howard from declaring the story until Clio was settled. An idea that she should go and visit the lawyer and ask him for details of the connection and perhaps information on Mrs Howard herself did cheer her slightly. He might provide a solution, for, at that moment, she could not really see one herself.

4

All three ladies were too tired by their journey to converse when they eventually reached home that night. Mrs Harcourt had been concerned about the quality of the posting inns on their route and had been determined not to put up at an inferior hostelry if this could be avoided for, as she explained to her daughter and niece, 'there could well be bugs in the beds or damp sheets to say nothing of ill-prepared food that might upset my digestion.'

Dorothea had ventured a protest. 'There are some excellent inns now, Aunt Sophie, that cater for the highest nobility and would certainly offer superior accommodation and meals.'

'Possibly, Dottie but I doubt that we could afford such places. Anyway, as I remember from the days I travelled with my dear husband, we always took our own sheets and at least two or three servants too. Oh dear!' She fumbled for her handkerchief and dabbed at her eyes at the recollection of happier days.

Fearing to upset her aunt further if she

pressed for a stop on their route homeward, Dorothea, who knew she could well have afforded it, gave in gracefully. It was therefore dark when they reached Harcourt Manor and they were all three worn out.

* * *

The housekeeper had prepared their rooms, aired the beds and had also laid on a cold supper to await their arrival. Aunt Sophie went straight to bed and had a tray sent up to her where, with the faithful Annie in attendance, she soon settled herself for sleep.

Both the girls attempted to eat in the dining room but Clio was moping as their holiday was at an end; also she was tired, so she only picked at her food and soon followed her mother. Dorothea tried to eat but found she kept thinking of a tall, dark-haired man whose eyes held such mischievous glints in their dark depths and who had roused emotions in her that she had never suspected she possessed. Eventually she decided that sleep was all she needed and she, too, retired.

Next day reaction set in. Clio continued to mope around the house and Mrs Harcourt remained in her room recovering from the ordeal of the journey. Only Dorothea attended to the household duties; she spent a couple of unrewarding hours poring over the accounts that had not been attended to in her absence. Harcourt Manor was a small estate with a few acres of parkland surrounding the house, while the home farm was let out to a tenant who, as part of his rental, provided them with all their dairy produce, meat and fresh vegetables. It was a successful arrangement, making the small household almost self-sufficient, which was a happy situation, since Mrs Harcourt's small capital had dwindled into almost nothing and only Dorothea's money now kept them all.

There was only one carriage left in the coach house. It was an old barouche that had seen better days, but which was used occasionally for visiting old friends in the neighbourhood now. The stables were much reduced. Two riding hacks for Dorothea and Clio lived with a pair of elderly animals that pulled the coach when necessary but none was prime horseflesh. One thing Dorothea had wished for when she first knew she had inherited money was a new horse for herself and her cousin for, fond as she was of their existing ones, she loved riding and hunting and both beasts were almost past such activities. Yet she had not bought new mounts, for her aunt would have worried about the money expended and the cost of their upkeep. It was another unfortunate consequence of being unable to declare how much money she had, for to do so would inevitably reveal the secret of the source, which had to be concealed.

Another day spent enduring Clio's moping and her aunt's less than cheerful countenance now that they were back in Bedfordshire made Dorothea risk broaching the subject of the London season again. She waited until they were all sitting down with their embroidery in the charming little salon that was her aunt's favourite room in the house. Dinner had been served and finished an hour or so before but there was still plenty of time before the tea tray would be brought in and they would retire for the night.

'Dear Aunt Sophie, do you think you could consider our removal to London for a few months now that your health is so much improved?' Dorothea began hopefully. 'We all so enjoyed our stay in Matlock Bath and London would be much more exciting.'

'Oh, Mama, do say yes, please do,' Clio begged. She dropped her embroidery, clasped her hands together eagerly and her lovely face lit up at the prospect.

'Well, my dears, I know you would both dearly like it but I have not got the funds available for such a trip. It would cost a great deal you know, and my poor dear husband did not leave a fortune when he died.'

Both girls contained their impatience as Mrs Harcourt wiped her eyes, but when the older woman said no more Dorothea went on bravely: 'I think that I could afford to rent a house for us, Aunt Sophie, and provide for us during our stay,' she ventured.

'You are so generous, Dottie, but we need your little income to run this house, you know.' Mrs Harcourt sighed. She was clearly tempted by the prospect but not convinced that they could manage to go. 'If we did rent a house it would not just be living expenses that we incurred either. A London season costs a great deal of money and you would both need so many clothes to make an impression. Then I don't know if I have the right connections any longer.'

'My lawyer, Mr Arnold, wrote to me while we were away,' Dorothea put in quickly, telling this small lie to help persuade her aunt. 'He said he had made some very successful investments for me with my capital and there is more money at my disposal than we had supposed. Do say that we may go to London and spend it there. Just think, dear Clio might find a suitable husband, for she meets nobody exciting around here.'

This was an argument that was likely to

sway her aunt, who adored her only child and wanted the best for her. With her hands folded over her sewing Mrs Harcourt nodded her head in agreement and her grey curls bobbed under her neat lace cap. 'That is so true, Dorothea. You could both find husbands, I hope, for you must remember you are now two-and-twenty, while Clio is still a girl and has years before we need feel she is on the shelf.'

'Oh, Clio will never be on the shelf, Aunt Sophie. All the fine gentlemen will be vying for her favours as they were at the Buxton assembly,' Dorothea rejoined with a laugh.

'Like James Sowerby,' Clio breathed. 'I do so want to meet him again, Mama, and he said he would be in London within the month. Oh do say we can go.'

Mrs Harcourt could never resist her daughter's pleading. 'Well, it might be possible, I suppose,' she murmured doubtfully. 'But it will still be very expensive.'

'I promise you, Aunt, that I can afford the money,' Dorothea said quickly. 'I must go and see Mr Arnold next week and he can make arrangements to take a lease on a suitable house for us and one or two servants.'

'Servants?' her aunt exclaimed, looking shocked. 'Oh we cannot afford more servants!'

'Just one or two,' Dorothea explained, realizing that she had made an error. 'We cannot take our retainers from here, for Crabtree, the butler, is too old and Mrs Edwards must stay to run Harcourt Manor.'

'Yes, of course,' Mrs Harcourt agreed. 'Perhaps one or two would make little difference and would probably come with the house anyway,' she added hopefully. 'Yes, if you really feel the lawyer is right and your income has increased it might just be possible, but we cannot be sure until you have seen him.'

'He will say yes, I know.'

'Oh Mama, how exciting,' Clio cried, getting up from her seat and whirling round the room. 'We can go to dances and balls, routs and supper parties. Why, we might even visit Vauxhall Gardens and see the Prince Regent. Oh, I can't wait to go. How soon can we arrange everything, Dottie?'

'Well, in a few weeks — maybe three or four,' Dorothea suggested.

Clio's face fell a little at this. 'So long! Oh why must we wait four weeks?' she wailed.

Her mother sat up straighter and admonished her. 'Do not be so silly, Clio. There will be so many preparations to undertake. First we must have some new clothes made up, for we cannot buy them all in London. Our little seamstress in the village will be far cheaper. Then I must write to one or two of my old friends and see if they will help me to launch you both. I know I may count on dear Lydia Garland — Lord Garland's widow. She and I both had our come-out together,' she mused thoughtfully. 'Then there is Alicia Deveraux. Mind you, I never really liked her for she has a spiteful tongue, but she could be useful and she was grateful to my father for introducing her to her present husband. It was at my come-out ball and poor Deveraux never stood a chance once Alicia spotted him, for he was a good catch but rather simple. Oh yes, Clio, there is so much to do. I must make out a list and I will write some letters tomorrow.'

'And I will visit Mr Arnold on Monday morning,' Dorothea said, growing nearly as excited as the other two. 'Oh thank you, dear Aunt. I am so grateful. We will have a wonderful time.'

'Oh yes we will,' Clio agreed rapturously.

'We should be grateful to you, Dottie, not you to us, my dear,' her aunt said seriously. 'If it was not for your inheritance then we could not think of such extravagance.'

'Well, you are my family and it is only right that I should share my good fortune with you,' Dorothea said impulsively, getting up to hug her aunt. 'You have been so good to me and, after all, I never knew the relative who left me the money so I don't even need to feel grief over the spending of it.' This was true enough for she had no clear recollection of her mother at all.

'Mrs Howard will have to wait to come and stay with us,' Clio commented as she sat down again. 'Unless of course we invite her to stay in London.'

'Oh no,' Dorothea and Mrs Harcourt said together.

'I don't think that would be suitable,' Mrs Harcourt murmured.

'No indeed,' Dorothea added. She had intended to avoid asking Mrs Howard by whisking them all to London and by no means must the vulgar widow learn where they had gone. The servants would have to be instructed to be very discreet. Exchanging a look of relief with her aunt, who shared her sentiments, Dorothea added, 'She could always come and see us later when we have returned, but no doubt she will be too busy to remember us anyway.'

The remainder of the evening passed in pleasant discussion of future plans, what they should buy in the way of clothes and other important and exciting preparations. The next two days were similarly occupied and the local seamstress came to the manor to take measurements for new dresses for them all. Dorothea wanted to set everything in motion before her aunt changed her mind.

She was also determined to find out just how much the lawyer knew when she visited him the following week. So it was with some determination and not a little nervous apprehension that Dorothea posted from Luton to London. She had visited Mr Arnold once before so she knew his direction and hired a hackney carriage to take her to Portugal Street, south of Lincoln's Inn Fields, where he had his chambers.

The young clerk who ushered her in seemed unimpressed by her old green woollen pelisse worn over a plain brown cambric gown, but Dorothea had dressed in old garments to travel on the public coach and cared little what he thought of her. Soon she would be able to enjoy many new gowns made by a London dressmaker in addition to the ones they had ordered locally and this thought sent her tripping happily into Mr Arnold's office.

The lawyer rose to his feet and greeted his client, smiling a welcome when he saw her face. She was not in the least like the other lady, who had been her mother and his former client, and with whom he had been a little in love. Dorothea Harcourt's brown hair was unfashionably styled, her drab clothes hid her figure but the shape of her face and her huge appealing eyes redeemed her and would, with a little town bronze, transform her into a very attractive young lady. However he remembered Melissa DeVine — she had dropped her married name as soon as she left her husband — and she had been enchanting. Her hair had been a glorious rich chestnut colour, her eyes — the only feature her daughter shared — deeply blue and her face perfect, while her figure had been voluptuous enough to turn even the staid lawyer's thoughts away from his papers. He sighed. All that was in the past. Melissa was dead, her reputation must remain secret, and now her daughter had come for a second time, presumably for advice.

'How are you, Miss Harcourt?' he enquired politely. 'I believe you have been visiting the Derbyshire spas with your aunt and her family?'

'Indeed we have. The Old Bath Hotel at Matlock which you recommended to us was quiet and pleasant — just what my aunt wanted.' The lawyer noted the word 'quiet' and the reference to her aunt. Clearly the younger members of the party had found Matlock rather dull.

'I am glad your stay was pleasant,' he

remarked. 'And now what can I do for you, Miss Harcourt? Do you require more money? You have drawn very little so far, you know. Most of your income is still untouched and the principal is very large indeed.'

'I know.' She sighed. 'I cannot spend much without arousing curiosity. Still, I have managed to persuade my aunt to move to London for at least three months for the Little Season in order to launch my cousin. I told her you had made some good investments for me and increased my income, which she believed, and so we can spend more.'

'Very sensible.' The lawyer, a man now in late middle age, crossed his hands on his desk and waited for her to continue speaking.

'I wonder if you could arrange a lease on a suitable house for us in a fashionable area with sufficient servants to run the place? We have only a few retainers whom we can spare from home to bring with us; just a groom and a lady's maid, I suppose.'

'That will not be difficult, my dear,' he said, showing some enthusiasm. 'I know of one or two houses that would be ideal. Perhaps if there is time we can go round and see them later today. You would like to examine and choose the property, I'm sure.'

'Oh, yes please, if I can do so,' Dorothea

exclaimed happily. 'I should be delighted to be able to go back and inform my aunt that the house is settled. She cannot change her mind then.'

'Is she likely to do so?'

'She is still concerned about the financial aspects of our trip — the expense of leasing a house, engaging servants and then the costs of entertaining, buying clothes and so on. I must take back an excellent report of my finances with me.' She smiled mischievously and Mr Arnold responded, finding himself enjoying their little conspiracy.

'That can easily be arranged, for your finances are excellent. If all my clients were as frugal as you, Miss Harcourt, I would have no problems to deal with at all. I can advance you enough funds for the initial expenses, which must include clothes and other items that will be needed before you reach London. When do you hope to come to town?'

'We have hardly been back from Matlock a week yet, so in about two to three weeks, I hope,' Dorothea explained. 'I don't want to rush my aunt too much.'

'Of course not. When you are settled in town do you perhaps have friends who can assist you in society?' he asked delicately. 'It is always so important when launching a young lady successfully to know the right people.'

Dorothea admired his tactful approach and was relieved to be able to inform him of her aunt's connections. 'She has already written to several of her friends, Lady Deveraux and Lady Farland are two,' she explained. 'Naturally she has not seen them for years since she has been living retired in the country, but she has corresponded and we hope that at least one will be willing to help us.'

'Good, good.' Mr Arnold actually rubbed his hands together in satisfaction. 'Excellent news. Lady Deveraux is very well connected and Lady Garland even more so and she has an amiable disposition too, so I've heard, which may be useful.' They discussed various points about the removal to London for a few minutes, then Dorothea began to twist her gloves together in her lap. Mr Arnold, watching her, was surprised by this sudden nervousness on the part of a young lady who always seemed to be calm and composed.

'Is there perhaps some other business you wish to discuss?' he enquired. 'Some problem?'

'Yes, there is,' Dorothea admitted, glad he had given her the chance to explain. 'It is about my mother.'

'Oh yes?' He waited.

'You told me very little when I first came to

see you but just explained that she had plenty of money given her by friends and had left it all to me when she died. I realize that since she left my father for a young man any mention of her would hardly help us now and you therefore counselled me to keep the source of my fortune a secret even from my family.'

'Your mother specifically requested that this should be so,' he corrected her gently. 'It was nothing to do with me. I was merely carrying out my client's instructions. Your mother wanted nobody to know of her existence or that you were her daughter. She did not think the English aristocracy would forgive her actions and she feared that their displeasure would extend to yourself.'

'I do understand,' Dorothea told him. 'I am sorry I never knew her, but I cannot feel that she cared a great deal for me, or she would not have left me.'

'She remembered you in the end,' Mr Arnold admonished. He wanted to think well of his former idol.

Nodding her head Dorothea agreed. 'Yes she did, and I have been most grateful. My aunt needed the money so I was happy to be able to supply it.'

'Then what is the problem?' he asked.

Again the girl fidgeted with her gloves

before plunging into speech. 'When we were in Matlock I was approached by a rather vulgar female called Mrs Howard. She claimed that she had been a friend of my mother's and that she knew her secret. She also stated that she would spread the story unless I co-operated with her.'

'Oh dear!'

'She insisted that we should take a trip to an assembly at Buxton. It was enjoyable, of course,' Dorothea admitted honestly. 'I'm not at all sure that it was quite the thing to do though, for Mrs Howard was not suitable as a chaperon and one gentleman pointed this out to me.'

'How unfortunate!' Mr Arnold murmured. 'Did this woman ask for money?'

'Not precisely, but I had to pay for the trip to the assembly and also for another expedition that she wanted to take. She then insisted just before we left that we should invite her to stay with us. My aunt was not at all happy about that, and I managed to put Mrs Howard off, but I am worried about what she knows.'

'I am not surprised. Oh dear! This is terrible. I cannot understand who she can be. Your mother was always most discreet and I am amazed that this Mrs Howard could have learned your name. Very unfortunate.'

'If she discovers that we are come to London and follows us she could ruin my chances of launching my cousin successfully,' Dorothea concluded sadly.

'She most certainly could. Also, as you have already paid for two trips at her orders she will hardly leave you alone now. When did she wish to come and stay with you?'

'Within two months. She was most insistent although both my aunt and I did our best to put her off. We live so retired I cannot see the advantage to her. She is a fashionable woman in a rather flashy way and wears many jewels.'

'Does she? Well, those might not be genuine,' Mr Arnold mused, rubbing his chin thoughtfully. 'Tell me all you can about her please, Miss Harcourt. I will try and find out what I can and make my own enquiries.'

Dorothea did her best to describe Samantha Howard and left out no little detail that she could remember of the widow's appearance or the remarks she had made. She sat back when she had finished, feeling very relieved to have shifted the burden to other shoulders.

Mr Arnold sat plunged in deep thought for several minutes. 'I will see what I can discover,' he said at last. 'I am puzzled by the resemblance she said she detected between you and your mother. It is only in the eyes that you resemble her at all and at first glance you are quite unalike.'

'Then she must have known who I was before she approached me,' Dorothea said sensibly. 'I had thought as much, yet where did she learn of me? Do you think it was from my mother?'

'It must have been,' Mr Arnold said reluctantly. 'Perhaps she was in your mother's employ at one time or other and pried into matters that were not her concern.'

Dorothea considered this quite a likely explanation and said as much. 'Could you tell me just a little more about my mother?' she asked wistfully. 'Where did she live? Where would Mrs Howard have met her or been in her employ? It was not in England, was it?'

'No indeed,' Mr Arnold agreed. 'Your mother removed at first to Europe with the young man she went off with, but he soon left her for other ladies and she had to fend for herself. She could hardly return to her husband and child, so instead she found another protector. It is not a new story, my dear, but for your mother it had a happy ending. Her new friend was a good man as well as being highly placed and very wealthy. He fell so deeply in love with your mother and she with him that theirs was an ideal relationship, only marred by the lack of a marriage to regularize the union.'

'Could they not have married once my father was dead?' Dorothea asked.

'The gentleman was too highly placed. I cannot tell you his name but he was of royal blood and his responsibilities necessitated that he have a wife chosen for him to bear heirs, so he was not free. However when he died he left provision for your mother of such a generous nature that she had no need to fear want ever again. She died soon after he did, of a broken heart, so I believe, and the bulk of this fortune has come to you. Your mother always followed your progress over the years, taking an interest in what you were doing. She knew you were being taken care of.'

'My father left me with his brother, as you know, and my dear Aunt Sophie has been just like a mother to me,' Dorothea agreed warmly. 'I have been very fortunate considering what might have happened. What would my mother have done if I had been in need?'

'Probably had you taken to her, but it might have caused difficulties. However, I am still concerned as to how Mrs Howard discovered your name. It is a puzzle that I must investigate.'

'I am just relieved that you know all about

it and will help me,' Dorothea said. 'I think that by removing to London within the month we may avoid the woman. I will see that the servants do not inform anyone of our whereabouts, so she may lose track of us all.'

Mr Arnold did not enlighten his client on how slim a hope this was. A woman as determined as Mrs Howard sounded would soon discover some trace of them and follow. He would have to investigate the matter himself and put a stop to her plotting if he could. He did not let the girl know his fears in case her pleasure in the coming London season was spoiled. Instead he suggested that if she had no more business to discuss with him they could take a hackney and visit the two houses he had in mind for her to rent in the coming months. Dorothea was delighted to accompany him and chattered gaily as they drove through the streets, for it was all still so new to her.

The first house, in Grosvenor Square, was rather too grand and at once the girl realized that her aunt would find the place so imposing that she would be in a continual worry over the expense, so she was grateful to see the second house. This was a much smaller mansion, though very elegant, in Arlington Street. Mr Arnold assured her it was just as fashionable an address and would suit them admirably. He hoped she would settle for this one as it was altogether more suitable. They went inside and Dorothea exclaimed in delight over the well-proportioned rooms and decoration. The furniture was as elegant as the house and the servants polite and helpful. So pleased was she that Dorothea agreed to take it on the spot and accompanied Mr Arnold back to his chambers to sign the necessary papers.

It was with a lighter heart that Dorothea posted back to Luton the next day after a night in a modest hotel, well satisfied with the outcome of her visit. She was tired but triumphant over all she had accomplished. Now they just had to wait for an answer to Mrs Harcourt's letters to her former friends and they could move up to London. Clio was in raptures and did not stop talking all evening about the marvels they would see and all they would do. Eventually her mother had to pack her off to bed, declaring that there was still a great deal of work to be done before they could leave the manor.

5

Their arrival in London passed in such a whirl that afterwards Dorothea could hardly remember what they had done. They seemed to possess very few of the items Mrs Harcourt considered necessary before they could go about visiting. In spite of the new morning and afternoon dresses made for them in the village, these were only suitable for use in and around the house in Arlington Street, she explained to them. Now that she had agreed to the trip Mrs Harcourt had found new energy and, remembering her own much earlier debut, had thrown herself into that of her daughter and her niece with enthusiasm.

She approved of the house as being just the right size, elegant and yet not ostentatious. She hardly noticed the discreet servants who came with the establishment, so enthusiastic had she become, and she was content to let Dorothea concern herself with the bills and the day-to-day running of the place.

The first few days were spent shopping for bonnets, gloves, slippers and accessories of every kind, and in the ordering of many more dresses for all three of them. For their visit to one of the most fashionable dressmakers, Madame Janine, they had Lady Garland to thank. Almost as soon as they had settled themselves into Arlington Street her carriage was at the door and she was being ushered up to the first-floor drawing room. She swept into the salon without waiting for the butler to finish announcing her and embraced Mrs Harcourt immediately.

'Oh, my dear Sophie, this is a wonderful day for me,' she enthused, removing herself from her friend's arms and dabbing at her eyes, which were suspiciously moist. 'I have been longing to see you again and now to have your daughter to launch into society and your niece. Why, I cannot think of anything I would rather do. We shall all have a splendid time, my love. Just imagine all the balls and parties. Thank you, thank you for asking me to help.' Mrs Harcourt had naturally found that she needed to wipe her own eyes at such a moving reunion but once she had recovered she set about introducing the two girls, who were watching the spectacle of the older women with great interest.

Dorothea had not quite decided which was the plumper of the two but thought perhaps Lady Garland was; this lady was certainly shorter and she moved with such speed she was like a whirling ball of silken skirts. Her grey ringlets were fashionably dressed and she wore a fetching bonnet of grey silk crêpe with lilac ribbons to match her grey-and-lilac-silk morning dress. She turned to survey the two girls and rushed across to Clio at once.

'You must be Clio. I thought so as soon as I set eyes upon you, for your mother had just such beautiful golden curls at your age. Lovely you were, were you not, Sophie? And your daughter is exactly the same. And this is your niece?' she queried, taking Dorothea's hands in her own small warm ones.

'Yes indeed. She has lived with us, as her mother died when she was four years old and her father passed on also, when she was only twelve,' Sophie Harcourt put in sadly. 'Poor child!'

'My Aunt Sophie has been like a mother to me, and Clio the sister I never had. I have been very fortunate,' Dorothea said quietly.

'Good, good. Very prettily spoken and I like you for it,' Lydia Garland said promptly, giving the girl's hands a squeeze. 'You are kind-hearted too, so I learn from your aunt's letters. It is your idea to launch your cousin, but I think we shall also be able to make a match for you too.'

'Oh yes, we must,' Mrs Harcourt insisted. 'If it had not been for Dorothea and her small inheritance I do not know what I should have done after poor Edward passed on.' She buried her face in her handkerchief.

'There, there,' Lydia Garland said affectionately, patting her friend's hand. 'We shall contrive very well but I do hope you have not written of your circumstances to Alicia. She does so love to tattle and nothing is secret with her. I believe she does so to make up for enduring Deveraux all these years. She has to have some fun!'

All the ladies laughed at this for Lady Garland's expression was so amusing.

Mrs Harcourt shook her head vigorously. 'Oh, of course I did not confide in Alicia. As if I would; I thought I should explain more fully to you, dear Lydia, but I merely wrote to Alicia to say that we would be in town for the season and I hoped to renew our acquaintance.'

'Very sensible,' Lady Garland approved. 'And now tell me your plans. What clothes have you ordered and do you know the right dressmaker to patronize? Come, we must put our heads together and discuss the details.'

So it was without more delay that the trio from Bedfordshire found themselves at Madame Janine's exclusive establishment, where they were treated with due deference. Lady Garland was an excellent customer and had been left very well off by her late husband. She supervised the purchase of several morning dresses each, formal ball gowns for the girls together with two afternoon dresses and new riding-habits for each of them. The first garments were to be sent round to Arlington Street in the next few days.

'So that you can begin to pay calls straight away,' Lady Garland told them as they returned laden with purchases. Dorothea had managed to take her aunt's friend aside and whisper that all bills were to be addressed to her and had impressed that lady with her shrewdness and good sense.

The meeting with Alicia, Lady Deveraux, did not take place until the following afternoon, and was less exhausting but also less amusing and entertaining. She was a tall, angular lady with a prominent nose and chin and piercing blue eyes that seemed to see right through a person. Both Clio and Dorothea found her intimidating, but she was cordial to Mrs Harcourt and affable to both the girls.

'I see you take after your mother in looks,' she told Clio, who had been struck almost dumb with awe. 'Very pretty but not too much brains. You'll do, I think. No doubt you expect to make a good match for her, Sophie. What is her dower?'

Before Mrs Harcourt could flounder into an answer Dorothea murmured swiftly, 'My cousin Clio has a sweet disposition and any gentleman will be lucky to win her.'

This remark succeeded in diverting Lady Deveraux's attention. 'Ah, you must be the orphan Sophie is sponsoring. Good of her, but unless you have a fortune you will have difficulty in finding a husband at your age.'

This rudeness did not please Dorothea but she gave no indication of her feelings. 'I am indeed most grateful to my aunt for all her kindness to me. However, it is more important for Clio to make a good match as I am aware that I am rather too old now.'

'Hmm. Well, you have good manners anyway, and a kind heart. Who knows, you might take. There is no accounting for gentlemen's tastes. Anyway, I want you all to come to a rout party at my house next week. I want to introduce you to society quietly at first, but of course all the *ton* will be there. My parties are always a success.'

Mrs Harcourt tried to sound grateful for this invitation and both girls exchanged dismayed glances behind the lady's back as she took leave of her hostess.

'Will Lydia Garland be there?' Mrs Harcourt enquired nervously, hoping to have some support from her real friend.

'Of course. Lydia goes everywhere. You were always a friend of hers, were you not? She never misses my parties. Well, I look forward to seeing you all. Come to dinner first and don't be late.' She sailed away down the stairs in the butler's wake leaving her audience speechless.

'Do we have to go to her house?' Clio asked after a moment.

'Indeed we do,' Dorothea said promptly. 'She would be most offended otherwise and you must meet as many of the right people as possible, Clio. If she does give important parties then we must attend. Is that not right, Aunt Sophie?'

'It is, my dear. You must excuse her manners. She was always abrupt and overbearing to make up for her lack of looks, I suppose. Still, she owes me several favours and I am sure that if Lydia is going we will enjoy ourselves. Why, it is in only four days' time,' she added, gazing at the heavily embossed invitation she was holding. 'Oh dear, I do hope your new dresses will be ready.'

'Madame Janine has promised them, so don't worry, Aunt Sophie,' Dorothea soothed. 'First we are to pay a morning call with Lady Garland tomorrow.'

'Mama's friend is such fun,' Clio put in

with a smile. 'I do hope the girls she is going to introduce us to are amusing also. It would be lovely to have friends of our own age.' Her wistful tone roused Dorothea from her reverie on Lady Deveraux's comments.

'Of course we shall like them and they us, especially you, Clio. Anyone Lady Garland likes is bound to be pleasant. Is that not so, Aunt Sophie?'

'Yes indeed. I am certain we will find the Mayland family delightful,' her aunt replied hopefully.

Accordingly the three ladies dressed with great care next morning. Clio looked enchanting as usual in pale-blue muslin embroidered with tiny forget-me-not flowers and trimmed with her favourite blue ribbons, while her straw hat was decorated with similar flowers. She wore a matching pelisse over her dress to keep out the fresh breezes. Dorothea had chosen pale yellow, which suited her brown hair but her long-sleeved dress was cut in a deceptively simple style and the high neck was trimmed with tiny rows of lace, as was the matching pelisse. Both girls felt very elegant. Mrs Harcourt was resplendent in crimson and complimented them both on their managing to look both plump and distinguished.

Lady Garland's carriage arrived promptly

at eleven o'clock and all three joined that cheerful lady as they set off. The Mayland family lived in Bedford Square in an imposing residence. The butler was so stiffly correct as he ushered them up the grand staircase to the salon on the first floor that the impressionable Clio was reduced to silence.

The gold-brocaded wall-coverings of the salon contrasted with white woodwork and the elaborate cornice around the ceiling was the height of elegance, as were the matching gold-brocaded sofas and chairs set around the room. However, Mrs Mayland proved to be a sensible and charming lady of Mrs Harcourt's age, and her two daughters were both a little older than Clio. One girl, Belinda, was only a few months older and, since she was extremely pretty with dark curls and bright-blue eyes, she provided a striking contrast to the other's fair beauty. These two struck up a friendship immediately and sat together on a sofa, chattering happily. The older ladies also seemed to be very compatible and it was left to Dorothea to struggle along with the elder Miss Mayland.

Angelina Mayland was also dark but not as pretty as her younger sister. She was nineteen, so she informed Dorothea, and soon to become betrothed. Her dark eyes were critical as they surveyed the visitor and she seemed to be assessing the style and cost of the other girl's outfit. Glad to be dressed in one of Madame Janine's new morning dresses, Dorothea endured the scrutiny and decided she far preferred the simple, fresh and unaffected Belinda to the more serious Angelina, who was very conscious of her own worth.

'When will your betrothal be announced?' Dorothea asked politely, as the conversation lapsed between them.

'Oh, very shortly I am sure,' Angelina told her confidently. 'The earl has been away tending to his estates but is due back in town any day now. He paid me marked attention when last he was in London and Mama is hopeful that he will offer shortly.'

'I am so pleased for you,' Dorothea said sincerely. 'We hope that my cousin Clio will make a suitable match while we are here and with Lady Garland's help to launch her I am sure she will do so.'

Angelina studied the fair head bent close to her sister's dark one and nodded rather disparagingly. 'She is tolerably pretty, I agree,' she murmured. 'With a good portion she could become popular. At least with her colouring she will not be a rival to Belinda, I am glad to say.'

'No indeed. They make a charming pair together. Do you go to Lady Deveraux's rout party in a few days?' Dorothea murmured, struggling to find a topic of conversation to interest this young lady.

'Of course,' Angelina told her. 'I am sure Rothley will be back by then and is bound to attend. You will see him there and many of the most notable members of society. Lady Deveraux's parties are always very select.'

This was good news but Dorothea was intrigued at the mention of Rothley. 'Who is Rothley?' she enquired at once. 'We have just been visiting Matlock in Derbyshire and spent a pleasant day at Rothley Hall whilst there.'

Angelina's face lit up with the first animation Dorothea had seen her display. 'Oh, Rothley Hall is the Earl of Rothley's seat in the Midlands. Did you meet him there? He is the gentleman I have just been telling you about — who is going to offer for me.'

'Oh, I see,' Dorothea murmured, enlightened at last. 'How exciting for you. No, we didn't meet the earl, only viewed the house and grounds. The housekeeper showed us round the mansion and we wandered at leisure in the gardens. The earl has commissioned a fine series of lakes, so we noticed.' The vision of the dark-haired man who had shown these to her came unbidden into her mind and excitement surged through her at the thought. So this girl was about to become engaged to his employer, the earl. It was very interesting and she hoped they could go on talking of Rothley, for Angelina might also know Mr Detherfield.

'Yes, I believe they provide a very pleasant prospect. I hope to see them shortly when they are completed. The earl has promised to erect a summerhouse especially for me at a suitable vantage point. I suggested a Doric-style temple, for I love all things Grecian, don't you?'

For some reason this made Dorothea's heart sink. So her advice to Mr Detherfield would not be taken after all if the earl intended to erect a temple for his bride-to-be. It was a pity, for the view would lose much of its charm with a building such as Angelina seemed to want. However she could hardly say so. Instead she murmured some polite response and was glad to see that her aunt and Lady Garland had got up to go. Dorothea had grown tired of the effort to make conversation with this dull and rather pompous young lady and she pitied the unknown earl, but she supposed he had chosen her himself and so must want such a worthy bride. She was not surprised to learn, on her way home in the carriage, that the Maylands were wealthy and had bestowed very generous portions on both girls.

'They needed to be generous for Angelina as she is such a dull child and so boring,' Lady Garland confided with a twinkle in her eye. 'Little Belinda is quite different and will take extremely well I am sure. She, too, makes her come-out this season with you, Clio.'

'Oh, she is such fun and we are good friends already,' Clio said impulsively. 'We are to go to the Pantheon bazaar tomorrow to choose stockings and gloves for the rout party. May I go, Mama?' she added appealingly. 'I would so love to.'

'Of course you may, dear, if they will take you up with them,' Mrs Harcourt said comfortably. 'I found Mrs Mayland a very sensible lady and her views and mine coincided on many subjects.'

'A very successful morning,' Lady Garland agreed. 'We shall make another call tomorrow, for it pays to meet people and become known, but Alicia's party will be the best way of introducing you to society. I also hope to procure vouchers for you to attend Almacks, so you must look your best.'

In no time, so it seemed to Dorothea, they were on their way to the rout party and, as Lady Garland had suggested, wearing new dresses from Madame Janine. Her own was, once more, of cream but of a pinker shade and decorated with coral trimmings that gave colour to her skin and made her hair glow a chestnut brown like burnished copper. She knew she looked her best but her thoughts were not on her own appearance, only on Clio's; the girl did indeed look enchanting. She was dressed in white with blue trimmings that brought out the blue of her eyes and the simple dress emphasized her dainty little figure to perfection. Dorothea was very pleased, as was her aunt. Clio would do them both credit and Mrs Harcourt was also looking very smart.

The house in Grosvenor Square was already filling when they arrived, to be greeted by their host and hostess. Alicia Deveraux was resplendent in purple satin. A huge turban added to her height, making her appear more domineering than usual. Her small spouse, on the other hand, was round and cheerful and totally under the thumb of his wife to whom he deferred at all times. The large salon where they all gathered before dinner was imposing, as befitted the house and Dorothea was amazed at the splendour of the dresses and jewels of the ladies. Her own simple row of pearls, like Clio's, were the most modest necklaces being worn. However, with the help of Lady Deveraux and Lydia Garland they were introduced to the thirty or so other guests who had been asked to dinner and were soon enjoying the evening very much.

The Mayland family was also present and Angelina took the opportunity to whisper to Dorothea, 'You will meet the Earl of Rothley later on. He was invited to dine but has only just returned from the country so will come on later. I am sure you will find him most distinguished.'

'I am sure I shall,' Dorothea agreed. Just then her eye was caught by a late arrival. To her surprise it was James Sowerby and her heart thumped with excitement. Maybe if he was here then Mr Detherfield would be attending also and she would have the chance to renew their acquaintance. She put out a hand and detained Angelina. 'The gentleman who has just arrived, who is he?' she asked softly. 'I believe I have seen his face before somewhere.'

'Oh, Lord Sowerby you mean? He too has been rusticating, I believe,' Angelina murmured in a bored voice. 'I doubt if you have met him but I'll introduce you if you like.'

Before she could do so dinner was announced and the party moved into the vast dining room. Lord Sowerby managed to take Clio's hand and bow over it and cause the girl to blush and simper with delight to see him again.

Dorothea had no chance to speak to Lord Sowerby himself as the dinner progressed, for he was seated some distance away and he spent the course of the entire meal, when not politely addressing his table companions on either side, in gazing at Clio, who also stared at him whenever she thought he was not looking. Dorothea was delighted that he was in town and that her cousin could meet him again. He had seemed such a charming young man and so suitable for Clio, but since they knew little of his prospects she enquired discreetly of the gentleman sitting on her right hand.

'I believe I have met Lord Sowerby when we sojourned in the Midlands recently,' she murmured as the first course was removed. 'Do you perhaps know him at all?'

The young man, Jonathan Portal, a worthy and earnest soul who reminded Dorothea of Angelina, smiled distantly. 'Why, certainly I know Lord Sowerby. Who in society does not? His family comes from Derbyshire, which is perhaps where you met him?'

'Yes, I believe it was there.'

'He is of a somewhat frivolous disposition, you understand,' Mr Portal went on, 'but well-connected, naturally.'

'He seems to admire my cousin,' Dorothea added thoughtfully as she watched James

Sowerby smiling across the table at Clio. She thought in surprise of the title he appeared to have. 'I hope he will not trifle with her affections, for she is so young and impressionable. He is not a fortune-hunter I hope?'

'Why, of course not!' Jonathan Portal exclaimed, sounding deeply shocked. His expression also displayed affront at her outspokeness. 'Lady Deveraux would never invite such a person to one of her parties, let alone her dinners. You mistook my meaning, Miss Harcourt. Lord Sowerby is eminently respectable, his family is of good lineage and I believe he has a comfortable fortune; although he is fond of fashion, which is all I alluded to. I am certain he means no disrespect to your little cousin.'

'No, no of course not. I did indeed misunderstand,' Dorothea said hastily, realizing she had shocked this worthy young man. 'I wish to protect my cousin, that is all, and in my desire to do so I was perhaps a little indiscreet. Forgive me.'

'Why, I quite understand your sentiments, which do you credit,' Mr Portal said rather more warmly. He studied the girl at his side more closely than before and decided he approved of what he saw. 'Lord Sowerby is very eligible but as yet no lady has captured his fancy,' he explained to her. 'He is certainly showing an interest in your cousin, which will do her no harm, I assure you.'

Much relieved by this, Dorothea tactfully changed the subject and they discussed innocent topics for the remainder of the meal. She made a good impression on Mr Portal, who found her intelligent and able to converse sensibly on many subjects, so that he was quite in charity with her when they rose.

On the other hand Dorothea had learned a great deal and was pleased that Clio had attracted the attention of such a suitable young man so early in their visit. If their attraction for each other continued, Clio might well make a match and Mrs Howard's threats would be meaningless. She was surprised to find Lord Sowerby titled and well-connected and wondered whether he was friendly with Mr Detherfield because he, too, wished to employ him. Then she remembered Mr Detherfield's spanking curricle and fine horses and wondered whether he was a gentleman fallen on hard times, who now supplemented his income by designing gardens for the wealthy. She would have to ask Lady Garland.

She had no opportunity to do so after the dinner for the party soon became too crowded and noisy. More guests arrived and Lady Garland whispered in passing that it was a most successful squeeze, an expression that summed up the crowded rooms. Mr Portal gravitated to Dorothea's side when the gentlemen rejoined the ladies and he gave her a commentary on the latest arrivals and their position in society. She knew that her enquiry about Lord Sowerby had produced this comprehensive guide but, after half an hour more of the gentleman's conversation, she found it difficult to stifle a yawn. He was worthy and respectable but so very dull. Even the knowledge that he found her attractive was of little consolation and she envied Clio the attentions of the handsome James Sowerby. It was useless to wish that Mr Detherfield had also attended but she could not prevent her thoughts from straying to that dark-haired, amusing gentleman whom she had last seen by the lakes at Rothley Hall.

Lady Garland bustled up to her and detached her from Mr Portal. 'Do come along and be introduced to Lady Jersey, Dorothea,' she said with a smile. 'She has promised to sponsor both you and little Clio and give us vouchers for Almacks. It is so good of her but she remembers dear Sophie, and of course Clio has been an instant hit this evening. Do please excuse us, Mr Portal.' She beamed at him.

The young man gave them a bow and

Dorothea gasped in relief as Lady Garland hurried her through the throng. 'Thank you for rescuing me,' she murmured.

'Yes, he is a bore, is he not? But at least he is of the *ton* so respectable,' Lydia Garland whispered back as she came to a halt in front of a fussily dressed lady whose sharp eyes took in every detail of Dorothea's appearance.

Lady Jersey, however, was good-natured and the girl found it easy to converse with her. She was still chatting with her and learning more of the company as Lady Garland moved on. Lady Jersey was known as a gossip and Dorothea found her amusing. She was diverted when Lady Jersey suddenly waved across the room to a gentleman just entering the salon.

'Dear Martin has arrived at last,' she cooed happily. 'He knows how to make an entrance. Poor Angelina has been waiting anxiously this past half an hour. You must meet him later on.'

Looking round to see whom she meant Dorothea's heart missed a beat and then began to race wildly. Just as she had hoped, Mr Detherfield had come to the party and now stood scanning the company from the doorway. Lady Deveraux rushed across to greet him and in moments he was surrounded. Lady Jersey turned to talk to another acquaintance and Dorothea was momentarily alone. She moved slightly so that she could watch the room from one side of an archway. Because of his height Martin Detherfield stood out above the rest. She gazed at the dark curls so artfully brushed *à la* Brutus, and at the casual elegance of his evening attire which reminded her so forcefully of the assembly in Buxton. Would he remember her? she wondered. She hoped very much that he would. She was rather surprised to find him so popular. Perhaps he had been employed by many of the nobility present and if so he must be a great deal more talented than she had suspected. She smiled to herself.

As Lady Jersey had said, Angelina Mayland was amongst those surrounding him and the girl's face was bright and smiling. Her betrothed should see her now, making up to another man, Dorothea thought, and gave a little giggle. She could understand anyone finding Mr Detherfield handsome but she wished he was talking to her and not Angelina.

Her wish was granted a moment later when he looked up and caught her glance across the room. At once he smiled and said something to the girl at his side. Angelina nodded her head and, as Dorothea watched, the two crossed the room in her direction.

With effortless ease Mr Detherfield managed to create a path through the gaily dressed throng and Dorothea's cheeks grew pink and her breath caught in her throat as sudden embarrassment at the prospect of meeting him took hold of her.

Angelina stopped in front of her and Mr Detherfield bowed. Looking up at him Dorothea saw his dark eyes resting on her dress; she sensed admiration and some amusement in their depths. Her shyness was forgotten as she acknowledged him, so that she almost missed Angelina's introduction.

'This is the Earl of Rothley, Dorothea. Sir, this is Miss Harcourt,' she said quickly with a little simper.

The smile on Dorothea's face vanished to be replaced by a frown. 'I beg your pardon?' she said, thinking she had not heard correctly. 'Did you say the Earl of Rothley?'

The amusement in the dark eyes gazing down at her deepened while her own colour grew higher. Angelina looked surprised and puzzled. 'Why yes, that is what I said. Did you not hear me? This is the Earl of Rothley, newly come up from Derbyshire.'

'Your servant,' Mr Detherfield said softly and bowed again.

6

All at once Dorothea felt cold and sick. Could this really be true? Was this man in front of her the Earl of Rothley? He was Martin Detherfield, surely, and he had told her so not once but several times. Then she thought of Mrs Howard's amusement and her chill foreboding grew. He had been playing a joke on her right from the beginning and now he was laughing at her openly. Filled with disgust both at herself and at him for the trick he had played she snapped her fan shut so fiercely she heard the sticks snap.

'Good evening, sir,' she managed to say and with a supreme effort controlled the quiver in her voice. 'If you will excuse me.'

Without knowing quite how she did so she left the two of them, moving swiftly through the press of people until she reached the door into the hall.

Briefly she looked around and saw the earl, as she now knew him to be, frowning. She realized that her departure had been unforgivably rude. Angelina Mayland would be most upset and offended, but as Dorothea fled upstairs to the seclusion of the ladies' retiring-room she cared little. How could he have been so heartless to call himself Martin Detherfield and to pretend that he was merely a landscape gardener? No wonder Lord Sowerby had seemed surprised both at the assembly and in the gardens at Rothley Hall. She had been totally deceived and knew herself for a stupid little fool. She had been taken in by a handsome face and polished address. He had treated her as no lady to begin with and his attitude later, at the assembly, took on a different light. She had so enjoyed their conversation but now she knew he had been teasing her, playing a game and laughing all the while at how gullible she was.

She sat quietly on the bed and slowly the sickness left her, but not the chill of self-disgust. Her dreams had faded completely during that introduction when she had learned the truth and her misery was now total; yet her good sense prevailed. She could hardly hide up here all the evening, for Lady Deveraux would be offended and her aunt upset. She could plead a headache — and in truth her temples were pounding already — but she had no wish to spoil Clio's evening. Her cousin was so happy and nothing should affect her if Dorothea could help it. Lord Sowerby, at least, had seemed sincere in his admiration for her cousin and she could continue to hope for a successful outcome there.

It seemed an age before her legs felt strong enough to support her and the flush had died in her cheeks. She made her way slowly back to the party and slipped into the room quietly, hoping nobody would notice her disappearance. At once Jonathan Portal materialized beside her and solicitously offered her refreshment.

Grateful for the lemonade when it came Dorothea sipped the liquid and listened to him discoursing freely on topics that interested him. She was glad that she only had to put in a word here and there to keep him talking happily. Some of her normal calm returned but she longed for the evening to end. Her throat was blocked with unshed tears and her headache very real. Relieved that the earl would never seek her out after her abrupt departure following their introduction she was unprepared to hear his voice and find him standing at her elbow.

'Portal, Lady Garland has just asked me if you would go and speak to her,' the earl said smoothly. 'I believe she wants your opinion on something.'

Smiling importantly, Portal bowed to Dorothea and moved quickly away, leaving her alone with the one man to whom she had no wish to speak. She moved to follow Portal, but not quickly enough. The earl put out a hand and detained her; without causing a scene she could hardly pull away.

'I think I owe you an explanation,' he murmured quietly so that only she could hear. 'I had no wish to distress you, Miss Harcourt, and I believe you were taken by surprise when we were introduced.'

'Indeed I was, Lord Rothley,' she told him coldly. 'There is no need for you to explain, however. I can understand your motives and appreciate that you enjoy a joke at another's expense. Now, if you will excuse me, I must find my aunt.'

'Not yet,' he said, still speaking quietly, but his hand tightened on her arm.

'Let me go,' she hissed, aware that her tears might spill over if she did not escape shortly.

'Only if you promise to listen to me,' he said and lifted his hand.

She did not move but held her head averted from him, willing someone to interrupt them and provide her with an escape. 'I cannot stop you speaking,' she muttered, 'but I wish to hear no more lies.'

'I have not lied to you,' he said harshly. Risking a glance at him she found the dark eyes were blazing with annoyance. 'My name is Martin Detherfield, as I told you.'

'You merely omitted your title,' she flashed, anger giving her back some of her courage.

'I never puff off my consequence.' His tone was haughty.

'Not even when I asked you,' she told him bitterly. 'I wish Mrs Howard had explained to me fully, then I would not have been taken in and thought you a mere landscape gardener. You have made a complete fool of me, Lord Rothley. May I congratulate you on a fine performance? I was taken in and believed you.' Spying her aunt in the distance Dorothea muttered an excuse and fled before he could restrain her again. She could take no more.

When her aunt caught sight of her white face she was at once all concern. 'Why, Dorothea my love, you look quite ill,' she cried. 'What is the matter?'

'Nothing at all, Aunt Sophie,' Dorothea managed to say. 'I have the headache, that is all. Do you think we might leave soon?'

'Why of course. I will fetch Clio at once. Do you go and get our cloaks and I will see the carriage is brought round. Oh, there is Clio.' She spied her daughter and James Sowerby near by and moved towards them just as the Earl of Rothley caught up with them again.

Turning her back on him, Dorothea hoped

he would take the hint. As her aunt was too agitated to notice she ignored him too. James Sowerby had seen what had happened and at once moved forward and took command.

'I will order your carriage at once, Mrs Harcourt,' he said. 'I see your niece is feeling the heat. Allow me to escort you.'

'Oh, thank you,' Mrs Harcourt fluttered while Clio took Dorothea's arm and led her from the room.

By now Dorothea was really feeling ill and even the fresh air outside hardly revived her. She heard murmurs of thanks and apology, knew Clio was fussing round her and heard Lord Sowerby promise to call on them next day. Then they were away.

Back in the salon the Earl of Rothley had watched their departure with very mixed feelings. He had observed the truly shocking pallor of the girl, and knowing he was the cause of her agitation made him extremely uncomfortable. When Lord Sowerby returned he at once grabbed his friend and demanded to know what had happened.

'You might tell me,' James Sowerby said promptly. 'I merely noticed that Miss Harcourt looked ill and that her aunt appeared upset, and I helped them to leave discreetly. Fortunately the company scarcely noticed, but I believe you were talking to

Miss Harcourt a few moments ago? Did you not see she was unwell?'

'I think it was my fault,' the earl admitted.

'So she discovered your true identity, did she?' Sowerby murmured and grinned but sobered when he saw his friend's expression. 'I guessed as much. Well, if you will pretend to be your own gardener what do you expect? I must say I think you played a shabby trick on the girl and I only hope her disgust with you will not make her cousin think the less of me.'

'Now who is being selfish?' the earl exclaimed.

'I am and why not? I have not been pretending to be someone I'm not.'

'Nor have I,' the earl muttered sullenly. 'I told the truth.'

'Up to a point.'

'Well, she wouldn't even let me explain.' The earl sounded aggrieved. 'I've never been snubbed twice in one evening before!'

'Do you good,' Sowerby told him roundly. 'I thought you were up to your tricks at Buxton and at Rothley but I didn't think we would meet them again so I let you get on with it.'

'Nor did I, but in spite of the row we have just had I think I will call on the family tomorrow. She interests me. Now come round to my house and share a bottle. This party has lost its savour.'

Nothing loath, James Sowerby followed his friend out, to the disappointment of many of the hopeful mamas present. The two men made their way back to his lordship's town house and Sowerby could not refrain from adding, 'I think that this time you may find your usual charm fails you, Martin, and serve you right. Miss Harcourt will not forgive you easily.'

'The challenge is even more appealing then,' Detherfield told him promptly. However he found himself left with a sense of guilt at his own behaviour for the first time in his thirty years and even after they had finished a second bottle of brandy he could not totally obliterate that feeling.

The night was even longer for Dorothea. She was grateful to her aunt and Clio for their concern but when at last they had left her and she could give way to her misery in the peace of her bedchamber she felt better. Her tears released some of her pent-up emotion and her head throbbed less painfully. As she lay and thought over the evening she came to the conclusion that the deception had been partly her own fault. It was not so surprising that the earl should have concealed his true identity from a chance-met girl who nearly fell under his carriage wheels. She could have been an adventuress for all he knew, yet that did not excuse him later. At the Buxton assembly he could have ignored her easily, since they were masked, but having sought her out he could have been honest with her. Nor could she forgive him for the deception he had practised at Rothley Hall, which had been truly unkind and unfair. She wished with all her heart that they had not gone on the expedition and she wondered whether Mrs Howard had planned for just such an event. The wretched woman had known his true identity and could well have intended to make capital out of it. Whatever the reasons she, Dorothea, had been stupid and gullible and the butt of a heartless joker. From now on she would concentrate on helping Clio to make a good match and forget her own wild dreams. She was too old to find a husband anyway, but Clio was different. Having made this resolve she fell asleep at last and woke with a clear head and only a slight pallor and misery deep inside as a consequence of the party.

Her family were delighted to find her so much recovered and all three discussed the evening's entertainment over breakfast. Clio was in raptures over Lord Sowerby and Mrs Harcourt thoroughly approved of the young man. 'He is so thoughtful,' she murmured to herself. 'Just what I would wish for my little darling.'

'Clio was a complete success and certainly the prettiest girl there,' Dorothea told them. Her cousin had no vanity and ignored the compliment, being too taken up with thoughts of James Sowerby. 'She has made a wonderful start to the season, Aunt Sophie.'

'And you were in fine looks also, my dear,' Mrs Harcourt told her affectionately. 'I noticed Mr Portal was greatly taken with you.'

'Have you made a conquest too, Dottie? Oh, that is marvellous,' Clio cried. 'Although I do not remember the young man. What did he look like?'

'Unexceptional,' Dorothea murmured drily, thinking of the dull Mr Portal with a deep sigh. It was a pity she had not made a conquest elsewhere but at least she would no longer cherish foolish hopes. She had been made a fool of once and would now wish Angelina Mayland joy of him.

They were all sitting in the drawing room when the first of the morning's callers was announced. Meyrick, the butler, ushered in Lord Sowerby and the Earl of Rothley and at once set Mrs Harcourt and Clio in a flutter. Dorothea wished herself anywhere but in the same room with the man who had made such cruel fun of her, but her pride came to her aid. She would not permit him to see her upset again, although she was surprised that he had bothered to accompany his friend.

When the customary polite greetings had been exchanged Lord Sowerby at once sat down beside Clio while Mrs Harcourt looked on fondly and fiddled with her embroidery as she attempted to make conversation with the earl. Dorothea had been standing near the window when the visitors were announced and she remained in the same position, taking little part in the talk, for she had no wish for private conversation with Rothley.

In spite of her lack of encouragement, which might have daunted a less confident man, the earl crossed the room to come to her side. 'I hope you are recovered this morning, Miss Harcourt?' he began politely.

'Quite, I thank you, Lord Rothley,' she told him stiffly. 'I was overcome by the heat, that is all.'

He regarded her thoughtfully. 'I think it was a little more than that. I want you to know that if I was in any way to blame I am really sorry.'

'It was nothing, sir. You reflect too much upon it.'

'Do I? I wonder. Well, I was certainly in

trouble with James and now you seem intent on keeping me at a distance. I can do no more than apologize, Miss Harcourt. You are a different person this morning from the girl I remember,' he added ruefully.

'As you are too, sir,' she snapped back furiously, feeling her colour rising in spite of her attempts at control.

'Not really,' he admitted. 'Although I might seem so. At first I was just being cautious when I spoke to a stranger on that day when you fell down, and afterwards it seemed a rare joke to carry on the deception. But perhaps I was wrong.' For him that was a great admission.

Dorothea did not regard it as such and merely murmured coolly, 'You were certainly wrong, sir.'

'Let us agree to forget the past and begin again,' he suggested. 'I have owned to my fault and apologized and I hope you will be magnanimous toward me.'

His smile was so charming that when she gazed up at him Dorothea knew she was relenting. He had apologized, after all, and he had paid a call to see how she was. To continue to be cold was churlish and she would only hurt herself in the end. She was about to agree to restart their acquaintance on a fresh footing when new arrivals were announced.

Meyrick threw open the door and ushered in Mrs Mayland, her daughters, and Mr Portal. At once Dorothea was reminded of the earl's imminent betrothal to Angelina Mayland and she turned from him immediately. She had so nearly been betrayed by his charm into making a fool of herself again. She moved away from him to greet Jonathan Portal with more warmth than she would normally have extended.

The earl was left alone to fume at the interruption and to curse the callers who had come at such an inopportune moment. He was so annoyed that he was at his most distant with Angelina and her mother. After his defection the night before the family was dismayed, seeing such a good catch possibly slipping away. Mrs Mayland made a determined effort to chat brightly to him, but she was received with monosyllables and she turned to Mrs Harcourt, hoping that her daughter would fare better alone.

Angelina, however, had taken a great dislike to Dorothea after her abrupt behaviour the evening before and now chose to vent her spite. 'Miss Harcourt's manners leave a great deal to be desired,' she remarked to the tall man at her side. 'First she rushed off last night and now she ignores us this morning. She must indeed be desperate to secure the attentions of Mr Portal.'

The earl had not missed the warm greeting Dorothea had bestowed on the pompous young man; it had irked him and aroused in him a strange feeling, which he refused to acknowledge as jealousy. He therefore objected strongly to this comment and said so. 'Miss Mayland, I believe you are misinformed. Miss Harcourt left us yesterday because she was unwell and had to leave the party early in consequence, which is why I am here to enquire after her health. No doubt Mr Portal has been kind enough to call for the same reason.'

Angelina realized her mistake and felt suitably snubbed. She said instead, 'I do hope you will be able to attend a little party my mama is giving at Vauxhall Gardens in a few days. We came to ask the Harcourts whether they could attend also; that is, if Miss Harcourt is fully recovered,' she added spitefully before she could stop herself.

The earl had been about to refuse, but on hearing who else was to be included in the party he changed his mind. When Mrs Mayland approached him with the invitation that he had overheard Mrs Harcourt accepting he did the same. Lord Sowerby and Mr Portal were still in the room so Mrs Mayland was forced to include them in the invitation too. Everyone accepted and the visitors all departed soon after, leaving behind an ecstatic Clio and a delighted Mrs Harcourt.

Dorothea was filled with a mixture of emotions. On the one hand her heart sang that he had bothered to come to apologize in person again, after she had snubbed him so deliberately the night before. It must show some regard, but then he was almost betrothed to Miss Mayland and had probably come only because his friend Lord Sowerby had suggested it. He had said that James had been annoyed with him and, as Lord Sowerby seemed intent on pressing his suit with her cousin, it was the most likely reason. Dorothea was still pleased to think they would all be in the same party for an evening's entertainment. Even the knowledge that the dull Mr Portal would also be in the company could not deter her from looking forward to the prospect, although she assured herself it was only because Clio's romance with Lord Sowerby might prosper.

The days between the rout party and the expedition to Vauxhall were pleasurably filled with calls, shopping and a musical soirée at Lady Garland's house. Dorothea had hoped to see the earl at this but although Lord Sowerby was there, dancing attendance on her cousin, the tall handsome figure of the earl was missing. She chided herself for her stupidity in wanting to talk to him again when he had treated her so shabbily, but she was nevertheless disappointed.

Again, when dressing for the Maylands' party she could not prevent herself from thinking of their coming meeting. She knew the earl was only going to be present because of his close ties with Angelina and her family, yet she hoped they could begin their acquaintance afresh as he had suggested. She wanted desperately to pretend his deception had never taken place, for he was such a charming companion and so much more interesting than any other young man she had met since their arrival in London. She would just have to remember that he was not serious if he sought her out, and to keep him at a distance even in her thoughts.

Lady Garland was to accompany them in her carriage; they would meet up with the Mayland family and the other guests once they reached Vauxhall. Both Dorothea and Clio were excited at the prospect of visiting this famous pleasure garden. Since it was to be a gala night they could expect a musical treat and truly splendid fireworks later on, so Lady Garland assured them.

The box that Mrs Mayland had reserved for the occasion was not very far from the entrance to the gardens. Situated in the first circle of boxes set amongst the trees and surrounded by brightly coloured lights, it was charming. The Earl of Rothley, Lord Sowerby and the Maylands were already seated in the box, watching the crowds passing in front when Lady Garland ushered in the Harcourt family. At once the men sprang to their feet and general greetings and compliments were exchanged. Dorothea sensed that the earl was watching her and she maintained her calm manner with some effort as she chatted with her hostess and tried to ignore him where he sat beside Angelina. Mr Portal arrived only moments later but Dorothea, after smiling a welcome, carried on her conversation with the older ladies of the party, for she had no wish to be monopolized by the dull little man.

However, the scene outside the box was far too entrancing for the younger members of the party to want to sit still for long. Sir Harry Fotherby had been invited; he was clearly enamoured of young Belinda and at his suggestion they all got up for a walk in the grounds.

Dorothea was not surprised when Mr Portal offered her his arm, nor that the earl was leading Angelina out, either. It was much as she had expected but her heart sank all the same. Clio was looking delightful as always and hanging happily on James Sowerby's arm while Belinda seemed as partial to Sir Harry as he was to her. The four of them walked off in one direction to see the fountains while the earl fell into step beside Mr Portal and Dorothea. Angelina gave the older girl a look of dislike and would have followed her sister but the earl ignored her tentative movements in Belinda's direction.

'Have you seen the octagon towers, Miss Harcourt?' the earl remarked, breaking across a discourse on the gardens that Mr Portal had launched into with little regard for that gentleman's feelings.

'No indeed,' she replied cheerfully, her spirits lifting as he spoke to her. 'This is my first visit here and it is all delightfully new and exciting.'

'You will find it tedious enough when you grow used to visiting here,' Angelina told her in a superior tone. 'It is also a little chilly this evening.' She shivered artistically, hoping for some solicitude from the earl.

She was disappointed in his reactions for he did not notice, or perhaps ignored, the fact that her shawl had slipped from her shoulders. Mr Portal, however, was far too correct to let a lady shiver in his presence. At once he paused and murmured, 'Allow me.' Adroitly the earl moved from Angelina's side to permit Mr Portal to arrange her shawl

131

more comfortably and, taking Dorothea's arm instead he moved off quickly, leaving the others still standing together.

'Are you in a hurry, sir?' she whispered, a mischievous smile breaking at the corners of her mouth in spite of her resolve to be serious with him. It had been a masterly manoeuvre after all.

'Of course. I cannot bear to be bored and we were both in danger of that if we stayed in Portal's company for long. He is a good fellow, naturally, but somewhat long-winded and fond of his own voice.'

Dorothea could not prevent a little chuckle escaping from her. 'He means well but perhaps you prefer your own voice instead, sir?'

'Aha. I see from that barbed remark that I am not totally forgiven yet. I suppose I deserve such treatment but did we not agree to forget our past differences?'

Dorothea pondered. 'You did suggest it, sir,' she told him truthfully. 'But I cannot be sure I agreed.'

'Then let us call a truce for this evening and allow me to show you the delights of the gardens rather than merely describe them. I think we can safely moderate our pace now, for we have quite lost our companions in the crowds.'

He sounded very satisfied and Dorothea,

since she was delighted to be alone in his company, gave herself up to enjoyment and refused to think how improper it was to be strolling along with another girl's betrothed in perfect harmony. The earl showed her the other circle of boxes, filled with gaily dressed gentlemen and their ladies. He pointed out the supper room and they listened to the orchestra for a few moments. Dorothea could have spent the entire evening wandering with him, chatting contentedly, but after an hour he reluctantly led her back to the box.

When they reached it they found the rest of the party already assembled again and only awaiting their arrival for supper to be served. Angelina glared at Dorothea: she was clearly furious at being separated from the earl.

'Where did you go?' she demanded, visibly demonstrating her jealousy. 'Were you indisposed again, Miss Harcourt?'

Embarrassed, Dorothea was about to reply when the earl answered for her. 'Not at all. I am afraid I took it upon myself to be a guide around the gardens for Miss Harcourt, since this is her first visit. I myself know them so well that it was refreshing to see them with another for the first time. It is a great pity we got separated from you but the crowds are so thick.' He waved a hand airily at the throng of people passing below the box.

Angelina was somewhat mollified by this explanation and Dorothea had to suppress a giggle in her handkerchief. She saw Lord Sowerby wink at his friend behind Mrs Mayland's back and knew that that young gentleman was not deceived either.

Mrs Mayland had bespoken supper for them in the box, preferring this to eating in the supper room itself. A lavish spread of cold meats, including the famous wafer-thin ham always served in the gardens, was laid before them to be washed down with fine wines and less potent beverages for the ladies. Conversation was general throughout the meal and the earl kept the party amused with lively anecdotes, helped by his friend. Only Mr Portal seemed not to enjoy himself. He had already whispered in Dorothea's ear as the supper was set out, 'I would have been happy to act as your guide, Miss Harcourt. I have an extensive knowledge of these gardens and the various changes that have taken place over the years. I even know the names of most of the performers who have appeared here in the past.'

Thankful that she had been spared this catalogue and had instead enjoyed a light-hearted evening Dorothea thanked him gravely and assured him she was sorry that the crowds had separated them so early on.

After the meal they all left the box to wander down to watch the fireworks. Once again the earl manoeuvred himself into a position next to Dorothea and she could not help being pleased, even if Angelina Mayland was on his other side. The display was magical and everyone clapped with pleasure when the last shower of golden sparks died away. It had been a memorable evening.

It was only as they strolled to the entrance to find their coaches that Dorothea had her first really unpleasant shock. She was being escorted by the earl and, as she replied to a remark that he had passed, she caught sight of a familiar face in the crowd surging towards the gates. Without thinking she clung more tightly to his arm and panic swept through her. Surely it could not be Mrs Howard here? The dreadful woman could not be in London. There were so many people; she must have been mistaken and imagined the overpainted face under the fair curls and green turban.

She relaxed slightly and hoped that if it had been Mrs Howard they had not been seen.

The earl noticed the increased pressure on his arm and looked down at once. He heard her falter in her reply and saw the anxious way she scanned the crowds. He was curious as to the reason for her behaviour, even as he felt a fleeting regret that it was not because of him that she had pressed closer.

'Is there anything amiss?' he asked softly.

'Oh no sir. Nothing at all,' she said, startled and scared that he had noticed her distraction. She flushed guiltily as she said this and his sharp eyes saw the blush in the glow from the lights twinkling around them. She was not telling him the whole truth but he wondered what or who could have agitated her so suddenly. When he handed her into the Garland coach he was resolved to discover just what had scared her so, although he saw that she had now recovered her composure and appeared her usual calm self.

The coach rolled away back to Arlington Street and Dorothea thought again of the glimpse she had had of Mrs Howard in the crowd. With a sinking feeling of despair she was sure it had been the lady and she determined to visit Mr Arnold or send him a message so that he could begin investigations here in the capital. He would know what to do. This resolve made, she tried to forget the incident and to join in the chatter on the evening's entertainment.

7

The next few days passed without incident. Dorothea had worried in the night about the glimpse of Mrs Howard but convinced herself she must have been mistaken. As she heard nothing either, she relaxed and decided not to bother Mr Arnold after all. It had just been a straightforward mistake on her part and some quite innocent person must have reminded her of the woman she wished to forget.

They were all too busy attending parties, musical evenings and even paid one visit to Almack's. This had assumed great importance in the minds of all the family and they had dressed with great care and arrived promptly for they had heard how the doors were shut at ten and nobody was allowed in after this. Dorothea found the evening rather insipid and the refreshments poor. She was delighted to find the Earl of Rothley, who was present that evening, shared her views, for he was of the same opinion exactly.

'I detest the weak drinks and even less appetizing food,' he agreed when she confided her reactions to the famous place. 'The music is unexceptional, the mamas too eager, to say nothing of the nervousness of so many young ladies.'

'Why do you come then?' Dorothea enquired innocently, but with a mischievous look up at him.

'Ah well, one never knows whom one might meet,' he told her with a raised eyebrow. 'Of course, it does my consequence good to be seen here now and again,' he quipped. 'I would have thought you of all people would expect that from me!'

Knowing she was being teased Dorothea felt her cheeks grow red but was determined not to let him have the last word. 'Naturally,' she responded. 'In such an exclusive establishment as this only the best landscape gardeners are allowed to enter, and you could find business, could you not?'

'I shall have a hard time living that down, I fear.' His expression was rueful but Dorothea saw his eyes were twinkling cheerfully and knew he still regarded the whole matter as a joke.

It was no use feeling hurt for she was aware that gentlemen of the first importance such as the Earl of Rothley had different standards from her own more modest view of life. It was still humiliating to think back to how innocent and stupid she must have seemed, so she changed the subject and the evening passed off pleasantly.

Once they had been seen at Almack's they were accepted and even more invitations poured in. It was delightful to be able to choose where they should go and Clio was finding many young gentlemen at her feet. But still she remained unmoved by any but James Sowerby. She danced with others, went riding and was seen in their company but no evening was complete for her unless Lord Sowerby was present. Both Mrs Harcourt and Dorothea began to entertain hopes that his interest was serious and Dorothea had to be very stern with herself to prevent a tinge of envy creeping in. She would have loved to be in the same position in regard to the Earl of Rothley. The more she saw of him the more she fell under his spell, but she had no intention of allowing him to know that she regarded him in a special way. She kept him at a distance, as she did the worthy Mr Portal and one or two other gentlemen who sought her company.

She had her second shock while on a drive in the park about three weeks after their arrival in London. The Earl of Rothley had arrived that morning to take her out in his carriage. Dressed in one of her most fashionable gowns of cream trimmed with green, Dorothea was in fine looks and very happy to be with the man she secretly adored. She had met him at many social functions but this was the first occasion upon which he had invited her to go for a drive. It seemed to mark a change in their relationship.

They entered the park just as a carriage holding the three Mayland ladies was about to leave by the same gate. Inevitably both vehicles drew to a stop and polite greetings were exchanged. Belinda was radiantly attractive and happily greeted Sir Harry Fotherby who came riding up on a chestnut gelding on the other side of the carriage. She was soon engaged in conversation with him, leaving her mama and her sister to a stilted discourse with the earl and his fair companion.

Dorothea could tell from Angelina's expression that the elder Mayland girl was furious to see the man whom she had hoped to marry in the company of another lady. It was understandable and Dorothea was reminded, uncomfortably, that she should not be encouraging the earl either, since he was so nearly betrothed to another. Mrs Mayland sounded cheerful enough in her greetings but her restrained politeness to Dorothea indicated that she shared her daughter's sentiments exactly but was more careful to keep them hidden.

Dorothea was relieved when a curricle coming up behind them forced them to move on in a flurry of goodbyes and insincere compliments on both sides. She kept silent for almost a complete turn round the park, for she was at a loss to know what to say and the encounter had spoiled her happiness in the outing.

The earl broke into conversation with a cheerful commentary on some of the notables who were driving round for the purpose of being seen, and Dorothea relaxed and contributed some comments of her own.

'Who is that gentleman with the little dog sitting up beside him?' she enquired curiously as they passed a smart phaeton drawn by splendid horses in which a rather florid-faced gentleman was sitting in state beside a curly-haired dog. 'He looks very grand.'

'Only in his own estimation,' the earl murmured in some amusement. 'That is Poodle Byng. You might have heard of him. He is an eccentric, which is quite the most fashionable thing to be. He was nicknamed Poodle because of his curly hair, then he took to owning one as well, so the name stayed with him.'

'To be different is to be eccentric, is it sir? I see. Then I suppose you would also come in that category as a designer of gardens.'

He gave her a swift glance from the corner of his eye and a rueful grin. 'To you, perhaps,

I might be eccentric but I doubt whether my peers are aware of my talents. Still, I thought you approved of the lakes, at least. You must give me credit for creating a fine vista.'

'And a Grecian temple, I believe,' Dorothea murmured softly. She had not forgotten Angelina's confidence regarding the temple to be built in her honour. She was pleased to see the earl frown and flick his whip in irritation so that the horses leapt forward, startled.

'Where did you hear that story?'

'Oh, from an interested party,' Dorothea replied innocently. 'I cannot say I approve of the scheme myself, but then my taste does not run to the classical. I prefer the rustic.'

'I have considered several ideas,' the earl commented. 'So far I have not made my final choice.'

He subsided into silence and so did Dorothea. His last remark was too telling. It sounded as if he had not quite made up his mind on the temple although he had said he liked her idea of an open view of the countryside. Did it also mean he had not settled finally on Angelina either? Or was it a polite way of snubbing her and telling her to mind her own business? She rather thought this latter view was correct and was despondent as a result. She almost wished she had not accepted his invitation to come out driving, for the more she enjoyed his company the fonder she grew of him and the harder it would be when he did become betrothed to the dull and dreary Angelina.

They had completed another half-turn before Dorothea caught sight of a very familiar purple gown and purple turban. Her heart sank and a cold fear took hold of her. When their carriage drew closer to the lady promenading on the arm of a young gentleman her fear increased. There could be no mistaking Mrs Howard's blond ringlets nor the flashy, slightly overdressed style she adopted. Even her jewels were too magnificent for such a promenade but more suited to a grand ball. Dorothea looked away quickly, tempted to hide her face in her hands but knowing that that would cause the earl to remark her behaviour. Even as she turned her head hoping the lady would not see her their eyes met and she saw a quick gleam of triumph in Mrs Howard's before the carriage had passed on and they were behind her. She had been even more shocked by the young man hanging on the lady's arm for it was, of all people, the pimply young fellow they had met in Matlock, Mr Simmonds!

Shivering with reaction and fright Dorothea turned to the earl. 'Could we please leave the park sir? I . . . I am not feeling myself suddenly. I have the headache.'

An observant man, the earl had noticed that something was amiss with his passenger. His eyes had idly taken in the overdressed female in purple and put her down as a vulgar upstart or perhaps a lady of the town, although the features had seemed vaguely familiar, as had the young man's. If his passenger had not stiffened so noticeably and turned away he would not have remarked them further; as it was he looked round quickly and saw that both had stopped and were gazing after his carriage. At once he recognized them and remembered where he had seen them before, but he could not understand why the sight of them had so upset Miss Harcourt.

'I am sorry you are unwell, Miss Harcourt,' he murmured thoughtfully. 'Are you sure it is the headache, for it is so sudden? It is not my company, I hope.'

'Oh no, of course not, sir,' she said sincerely and in her usual tone. Then, remembering Mrs Howard's expression she could not prevent herself from shivering again. 'However I do fear I am not myself and would be better at home, if you please.'

'Of course. I will take you at once. We can make better speed if we leave my groom here.' The earl drew his carriage to a halt and spoke a few words to his groom, who was up behind. That worthy jumped down at once and moved off into the crowd in the park while the earl took up the reins once more.

Dorothea was too bemused by the awful appearance of Mrs Howard in her life again just when things were going so well to notice this slightly odd behaviour on the part of the earl. She had visions of the woman arriving in Arlington Street and these filled her mind. Not only would the earl cease to visit, which was bad enough, but Lord Sowerby would stop pursuing Clio and all her hopes of a fine marriage for her cousin would be dashed. How could she stop Mrs Howard from spoiling everything for them? Now she would *have* to consult Mr Arnold and perhaps prepare to bribe the woman with half her fortune so that at least Clio could become well established.

The drive back to Arlington Street was swift but for once Dorothea wanted to be free of the earl's company so that she could think about this new disaster. It must indeed have been Mrs Howard that night at Vauxhall, and now there was no way she could hide. Recognition had been mutual and instantaneous.

'Miss Harcourt, we have arrived,' the earl

said patiently. He had brought the carriage to a halt outside their front door and was now standing in the street waiting to hand her down.

'I am sorry, sir. I had not noticed,' Dorothea apologized. 'I was woolgathering.'

'Yes of course. The headache,' he said kindly, but as she glanced up she saw from his expression he did not believe her excuse. 'If there is anything I can do to help?' he suggested. 'I would be delighted to be of service.'

A faint flush stained her cheeks at his thoughtful concern which, she sensed, was genuine; yet he, of all people, must never learn the truth. He had deceived her, certainly, but his deception was as nothing to her own. When she thought of her mother and what society would make of such a scandal she shuddered again. It was too dreadful to contemplate. 'I thank you, but it is nothing, Lord Rothley.' She had grown formal in her distress. 'You are too kind but I shall be well directly. It is nothing.'

'As you wish, Miss Harcourt,' he said in a reserved tone. He watched her mount the steps and enter the house without a backward glance. Unused to being ignored by any female, particularly one on whom he had bestowed flattering attentions, the earl sighed. Instead of being annoyed by her attitude he was both bemused and faintly worried. She was clearly upset and not by something like a headache, yet she would not confide in him; so he would have to discover what was amiss for himself. Any information that his groom might discover on following the two in the park could prove useful. Also James Sowerby might have learned something of the family's background that might give a clue, for Clio prattled artlessly and kept no secrets. Decidedly it was worth talking to his friend. He leapt up behind the horses and gave them their heads as he drove off to White's to find him.

The atmosphere in White's was comfortably masculine. The faint smell of rich wine mingled with tobacco and the murmurs of gentlemen's voices. At first the earl did not see his friend and wondered whether he had made a mistake and Sowerby was socializing or perhaps working out in Gentleman Jackson's boxing saloon. Then he spotted him talking with two other cronies in a corner. He strode across and interrupted them with ruthless disregard for civility.

When he had prised James Sowerby away and both had settled comfortably at a table far from their fellows with a bottle of good claret, James broke into speech. 'You were very high-handed a moment ago, Detherfield,' he said, rather annoyed by the earl's arbitrary dismissal of his friends. 'What do you want with me that cannot wait even a few minutes?'

'I'm not sure,' the earl told him slowly. He sipped his wine and frowned in concentration.

'Well really, Martin! Are you foxed or something? It's a bit early in the day for that and anyway I thought you were taking Miss Harcourt out driving.'

'I'm not foxed and yes I have just returned from the park with Miss Harcourt.'

'You were quick. Did she rip up at you again, then? I told you she would never fall for your charm after the tricks you played on her,' Sowerby said cheerfully. Then he noticed how serious the earl looked and his manner changed. 'Something is up old fellow, is it not? Tell me?'

The earl did so, describing the incident in the park and Miss Harcourt's reactions. 'She was very upset at the sight of this woman, which surprised me because she and her sister were being chaperoned by the woman in Buxton.'

James Sowerby was less interested in the woman than the man. 'You mean that pimply pipsqueak is back in town?' he exclaimed in indignation. 'I hope he keeps away from Clio — or Miss Harcourt, that is. I'll call him out if he dares to insult her again.' He had heard all about Mr Simmonds's manhandling of the lovely girl at the assembly from his friend.

'Steady on. Don't get excited,' the earl told him mildly. 'I think there is a great deal more behind this than we know. As you also are interested in the family we should try and discover what is amiss.'

'I am interested in the younger Miss Harcourt, certainly,' James Sowerby agreed promptly. 'I intend to try my luck and propose. I decided last night,' he admitted in a burst of candour.

'Congratulations, James,' the earl said, slapping his friend on the back. 'I think you will suit one another very well. Mind you, she's not very long on brains, you know.'

Sowerby waved his glass. 'I don't care for clever women, Martin — never did. She is lovely and good and kind and has the disposition of an angel and — '

'Yes I know, I know,' the earl cut in impatiently. 'Come back to reality. The family is possibly in some kind of trouble and we must discover what it is. Has the gorgeous Clio given you any hints on scandals in her past?'

'Not at all.' Sowerby sounded affronted at the suggestion. 'There can be no scandals. She is pure and above reproach and so is her mother. Her father has been dead three years,

I believe, and they are none too plump in the pocket, but that is all that is amiss, I am sure.'

'Well, if she knew anything she would tell you. She is not the type to keep a secret,' the earl agreed. 'Still, I am surprised when you say they are short of money, for they display reasonable wealth at present and I have heard it rumoured that one of them is an heiress.'

'Oh, such rumours always spread about new arrivals when little is known of the family, but their birth and connections are excellent,' Sowerby told him. 'I had it from Clio that her cousin helps the family finances and that but for her they would be almost destitute, as Clio's father left little. He was a gambler, of course, but the cousin has a small inheritance and has also financed this London season.'

'Has she indeed? I was not aware of that.' The earl was irritated that he knew so little about Dorothea and that even his friend had apparently learned more. She had been keeping him at a distance, to be sure.

'What is your interest in all this, Martin?' Sowerby enquired curiously. 'You know mine, for I have made no secret that I love Clio and hope to make her my wife, but you are different. You might have amused yourself teasing the older one, but I thought you had paid her a few attentions since their arrival in town merely to make up for your past tricks. After all, everyone expects you to offer for Miss Mayland, you know.'

The earl scowled into his glass. 'I know and I don't intend to oblige them, either. The girl is a bore, dull — and spiteful too,' he added, remembering her attack on Dorothea.

Very puzzled by this change of heart Sowerby murmured, 'But you were dangling after her before you retired to Derbyshire for the summer. Bets were laid on whether or not you would make a match of it before you departed. The Maylands expected it daily — and still hope, naturally.'

'I have changed my mind,' the earl said stiffly. 'We will not suit at all. I have made no promises and I have not distinguished her with attentions this last month. She cannot accuse me of misleading her.'

Sowerby drained his glass and poured another thoughtfully. 'I can't say I blame you, old fellow. Never did think much of her. The younger sister Belinda is a far more fetching little piece, though not my style. Still, they did hope to bring you to the altar, though I admit the odds have lengthened now on her succeeding in leading you there. Who is going to be the lucky girl, then? I thought you wanted an unexceptionable wife to set up your nursery.'

'So did I, but now I think that maybe I have been caught by my own follies.'

'The trickster tricked, eh?' James Sowerby murmured. 'Well if I can help, old fellow, I will do so, but I have told you all I know of the Harcourt family. Seems respectable enough but maybe you should enquire into your Dorothea's parents. Who were they? Do you know that?'

'No, I don't and I think you could be right, James. I will look into that right away. Now, if you will excuse me, I think I'll pay my maternal grandmother a little visit. She is getting on but remembers everyone and any scandal or titbit in the past is meat and drink to her. She will know if anyone does. Excuse me.'

'Hey, old fellow, you haven't finished your drink,' Sowerby exclaimed. 'There is still half a bottle!' But the earl had gone and Sowerby picked up the remains and retired to join his cronies again.

Meanwhile Dorothea had sought the sanctuary of her bedchamber. The disastrous encounter in the park had driven even the embarrassing meeting with the Maylands right out of her mind. She had no doubt that Mrs Howard would seek her out quickly, but it was difficult to be certain of what that lady would demand. She dreaded such a meeting, yet almost wanted to get it over so that she knew the worst. On reflection she decided not to tell her aunt that she had seen Mrs Howard again, nor did she intend Clio to learn that Mr Simmonds had been in her company. It was surprising that they knew one another, and not in the least reassuring.

When she had heard nothing by the next morning she took her aunt's carriage and made a quick visit to the lawyer. Mr Arnold was horrified, sympathetic and promised help. She left his office somewhat reassured but still very worried about her own and Clio's future.

She had begun to relax a little when several more days passed without incident. No note was delivered nor did she see Mrs Howard again, although she went driving in the park on two more occasions with the earl. He made no reference to her abrupt return home on the occasion of their first drive and nor did she. Once more they enjoyed verbal sparring matches, during which Dorothea concealed her growing affection for him and kept him at a discreet distance while benefiting from the esteem his escorting gave her in the polite world.

The earl, too, had no wish to bring up the subject yet. His own investigations were progressing in an interesting way and while

153

Dorothea Harcourt did not confide in him he would not force her into an embarrassing disclosure. When he was certain of the facts he intended to deal with matters himself.

Thus it was that Dorothea, accompanied only by the maid Annie, took the carriage to make a few small purchases and to exchange her aunt's books at the circulating library. Mrs Harcourt had little time or energy to read with all their social engagements but she liked to have the latest books in the house so that she could make suitable murmurs when the plots were discussed during morning calls or over the tea-tray.

Dorothea emerged from Hookhams in Old Bond Street well pleased with her selection. She had obtained the latest Gothic romance for her aunt and knew that that lady would be delighted. Her mind was busy working out how many yards of blue silk ribbon she needed to trim a dress for Clio so that it could be transformed and worn again. She also wanted some silver netting to go over a ball gown of her own to give it a completely new and up-to-the-minute look. In spite of having spent so much on new outfits she and Clio also made over several other garments and were clever enough to disguise their handiwork from all but Mrs Harcourt, who approved of such economy.

'I think I will visit Grafton House for fabrics, Annie,' Dorothea murmured as they walked over to the carriage. 'They have such a fine selection.'

'Perhaps I can accompany you,' a voice murmured in her ear before Annie could reply.

Dorothea paused on the pavement, startled and horrified to hear the very accents she had been dreading for so many days. Annie fell back a few paces to give Mrs Howard room to stand beside her mistress. Mrs Howard was indeed resplendent in a walking-dress of china crêpe in a rich pink shade, trimmed with cream silk ribbons and topped by a velvet jacket in the same pink shade. She looked opulent, plumper than ever and vulgar to Dorothea's critical eyes.

'Mrs Howard, how pleasant to see you again,' Dorothea greeted her when she had recovered her composure sufficiently to speak. 'I am afraid we are in rather a hurry now, so perhaps we can meet some other time.' She beckoned to Annie and tried to walk past the other lady but in vain.

Moving fast, Mrs Howard anticipated her and positioned herself between the young woman and the carriage. Short of creating an unpleasant scene there was little Dorothea could do.

'I would like you to take me up with you, my dear,' Mrs Howard said smoothly. 'We have so much to discuss since our last meeting. Perhaps you could send your maid home with your books and we could take a turn round the park in your carriage? I am delighted to see it is a barouche, so the coachman will not be able to overhear us and we can be private together.'

Her words were spoken politely but Dorothea sensed underlying menace and knew she had to comply and find out what the woman wanted. She had been expecting something of the sort, after all. She instructed Annie to return to Arlington Street without her, then she climbed into the barouche after Mrs Howard with as much grace as she could manage.

Once seated in the carriage as it moved along the busy street Mrs Howard did not rush to speak. It was Dorothea who anxiously broke the silence between them. 'What is it you want, Mrs Howard? Why do you insist that we have matters to discuss? I have nothing in common with you at all.'

'That is plain speaking indeed, my dear, but it will do you no good,' Mrs Howard said cheerfully. 'I know you wish me anywhere but in London and I suppose you thought you had escaped me by leaving your estate in

Bedfordshire. I have ways of finding out information and I have been watching you since I caught a glimpse of you at Vauxhall Gardens. So lucky that was for me.'

'What do you want?' Dorothea said again, biting her lip in agitation. Would the wretched woman never come to the point?

'I have various plans but I am not sure which one I fancy following yet,' Mrs Howard murmured.

'If you want money you can have it if you will leave us alone,' Dorothea said bluntly in desperation. 'My cousin Clio is on the point of a good match and I want nothing to spoil it.'

'Well, that is just the problem, my dear. You see, my nephew has a *tendre* for your cousin and I am not sure that it wouldn't be in his best interests if I disclosed your reputation so that your family would be shunned by the *ton* and he could have the girl.'

'Your nephew?' Dorothea was puzzled, then she remembered seeing Mr Simmonds hanging on Samantha Howard's arm in the park. 'You mean Mr Simmonds, I presume?'

'I do indeed. The poor boy is so smitten I can hardly keep him in check, and of course you must appreciate an aunt's tender feelings.' This was such an appalling twist of fate that Dorothea was reduced to silence for a full minute. What on earth could she do now? Clio's future was of the utmost importance but she knew that London society would never countenance the family once her mother's secret was out. Even Lord Sowerby's devotion could not be expected to continue.

At last she managed to say quietly, 'I think that would be ill-judged, ma'am. My cousin is not a practical young woman and would never be able to hold household successfully unless there were a large income for servants.' This was not altogether true, but Samantha Howard did not know it. 'Does your nephew have a fortune?'

Mrs Howard frowned slightly. 'Not at all, but then you do, do you not? With your money they could be set up nicely.'

'Possibly, but once you have declared my family secret there is no reason why I should give you a penny piece, and I will not,' Dorothea said firmly.

Her bluff gave the woman pause to think. 'I did wonder about that myself,' she muttered. 'Well, I have other plans, so we can forget your cousin. Poor dear Tom will have to find himself another girl. There are plenty around and he will forget in time.'

Breathing a sigh of relief Dorothea unclasped her hands, which had been tightly pressed together. 'What is it you want then, madam?

Money, I gather, to keep you in comfort.'

'I did think of money, certainly,' Samantha Howard admitted. 'Particularly when I first approached you, for I knew how much your dear mother had left to you. You are indeed an heiress, although unable to claim that distinction.' She tittered unpleasantly behind her glove. 'Still, never mind that now. I have observed the high society in which you move and I have devised other plans. I see that the Earl of Rothley is interested in you and has been escorting you assiduously. Such a charming man, our Mr Detherfield.' Again she tittered and Dorothea longed to slap her painted face. Instead her own colour rose and she knew that the woman had noticed her reaction.

'Oh, fond of him, are we? I'm not surprised. Well that is all to the good because my third plan is undoubtedly the best. I think he will propose to you, my dear, for he intends marriage and has done for months.'

'Nonsense, ma'am. You are misinformed.'

'Oh, I think not. He needs to set up his nursery, for he is past thirty,' Mrs Howard said smugly.

'I did not mean about his intentions regarding matrimony, but that he will propose to me. He is merely amusing himself with me as an extension of the deception he practised over his name when in Derbyshire. Which you knew all about,' she added accusingly.

Mrs Howard preened herself as she sat back against the rather drab brown squabs of the coach. 'Yes, I did know what he was up to, but I thought it so amusing and I was not sure if it might not be to my advantage to keep you in ignorance. And so it has proved. For whatever you say, my dear, the earl has shown you a marked interest. It is being commented on all over town.'

Dorothea was scarlet by now with rage and mortification. How dare this woman address her so? 'I dislike such speculation, ma'am and discount it entirely.'

Her cool tone did not deceive the other woman. 'Say what you will, I think you are mistaken. Wait and see, my dear.'

'How can I with you threatening exposure?' Dorothea demanded.

'Well, that is just the point I intend to make.' Mrs Howard leaned forward and placed her warm hand on the younger woman's knee. Dorothea did her best not to shrink back in revulsion. 'When the earl proposes you accept him, and when you are married you can introduce me into society and find me a rich old widower. I am as in need of setting up for life as you are, for we are neither of us getting any younger.'

This comparison between them was so

ludicrous that Dorothea would have found it amusing if she had not been so distressed. 'I suppose you would spread the scandal if I refused to launch you once I was married, and so ruin my husband too,' she said quietly. 'What a despicable trick.'

Samantha Howard laughed and patted her fair curls. 'Not at all. A woman like me has to live by her wits and I win on every count, for if the earl does not propose to you then you can give me the money to keep quiet and so at least console yourself with your cousin's good fortune and marriage. I prefer the thought of a secure future but sufficient money will ensure a good lifestyle for Tom and myself until I find another husband. Oh yes, I think I will do very well out of this. I am so glad I met and recognized you, my dear. I had been hoping to discover Melissa's long-lost child and when I saw those great blue eyes of yours I had no doubts at all. Now, you can set me down here but don't think I shall disappear. I shall be back to claim my money or even better my launch into society. It is up to you which it will be but the earl is a charming man and a future with him could be very pleasant for you.'

Instinctively Dorothea tapped on the window to stop the coach. She watched Mrs Howard alight and for once offered no assistance. Let her fall if she would. The woman's last remarks had hurt deeply. There was nothing Dorothea would like better than to marry the earl, and to hear that his interest had been noted and remarked on made her heart beat faster. Yet in view of what Mrs Howard had threatened there could be no possibility of her marrying him. It would be too cruel to do such a thing to him if exposure could follow, and she cared too much for him to run such a risk. Also her own secret shame in her mother's background must always preclude such a match. Mrs Howard had merely made it entirely impossible. If the woman would accept money then at least Clio could be happy. There was no immediate danger of exposure, for it was not in the woman's best interests to precipitate matters.

This crumb of comfort was all Dorothea had to cling to as the coach trundled back to Arlington Street, where she hoped to give way to her misery in the privacy of her bedchamber.

8

However even this comfort was denied her. She had hardly entered the house before she knew that something had happened. The butler was shaken out of his usual impassive calm and informed her loftily that her aunt was entertaining guests in the green salon and desired her presence as soon as possible.

His pompous description of the pleasant room on the first floor where they received callers would have made Dorothea smile on any other day. As it was she merely sighed and tried to collect her thoughts.

'All right Jenkins. Tell my aunt I will be with her directly when I have tidied myself.' The girl made her way slowly up to her bedchamber and looked longingly at the bed. She wanted to lie down and forget all that had happened, the ruination of hopes she had been secretly cherishing, but it was not to be. She knew now that her hopes had been ridiculous, because she realized that she could never marry at all. Any man would be horrified to learn what her mother had done; would never offer for her if he knew, and if discovery occurred after marriage two lives would be ruined instead of one. She had refused to acknowledge this to herself and certainly not since she met Martin Detherfield, Earl of Rothley. He was the man of her dreams brought to life, and to have heard Mrs Howard talking of his interest in her had only made her position seem more wretched. Wildly Dorothea wished for a moment that Samantha Howard could be crushed under a carriage, but her mama's secret would still exist and could not be told without arousing a disgust of her in any suitor.

She made her way down to the first floor and hoped that her pallor would not be noticed by her aunt and the callers. She had pinched her cheeks, vainly, to try and produce some colour but she knew she was not in her best looks. When she opened the door she was at once aware of what must have taken place in her absence.

Clio and Lord Sowerby were seated together on a sofa. Her aunt was comfortably settled in her favourite chair with a piece of her embroidery resting on her lap; she was looking bemused with happiness.

At her entrance Clio jumped to her feet and rushed across the room to fling her arms round her cousin, while Lord Sowerby got up and Mrs Harcourt dropped her embroidery as she turned in her chair.

'Oh Dottie! Dottie! Just imagine it! Lord Sowerby — James — has asked me to marry him!' Clio explained when she had finished hugging her cousin. 'Is it not the most wonderful thing that has ever happened? I am so happy I do not know what to say.'

Dorothea was delighted for the couple and told them so immediately. James Sowerby looked greatly pleased with himself as he gazed dotingly on Clio; for once his fluent address had deserted him. His sincerity was obvious and Dorothea's spirits rose when she thought that at least Clio would be honourably settled. Once she had married she could disclaim kinship if Dorothea's secret ever did get out and it would not touch her in the same way at all. Relieved now that Mrs Howard had decided against her first plan, to secure Clio for her horrid nephew, Dorothea joined in the congratulations, picked up her aunt's sewing and wisely placed it out of reach on a side table before ordering champagne to celebrate.

They were sipping the cool wine brought promptly by the smiling Jenkins, who had been waiting for just such a summons and knew exactly what had occurred, while Clio chattered on about her plans. Lord Sowerby smiled fatuously and Mrs Harcourt twittered happily.

'We are to give a party in three days to celebrate,' Clio explained. 'Will that not be wonderful? I will help you with the invitations and arrangements, Dottie. Oh, I am the luckiest girl in the world.'

Secretly Dorothea agreed with her. The future did indeed look rosy for her lovely cousin. Clio could be married just before the festive season commenced, as Lord Sowerby wished to make her his own before anyone could snatch such a prize from him. Although this would allow them less than two months to prepare, Dorothea was delighted with the scheme. A prompt wedding would ensure that Mrs Howard and her plans could not interfere with Clio's happiness. It was an excellent idea, although Lord Sowerby did say that if his darling wished she could complete the season first and be married in the spring. Clio was too happy to care for such a delay and since she had found the man she loved already what was the use of waiting longer? They could return from their honeymoon to enjoy a further round of parties and balls as a married couple if he wished.

At this point Dorothea had had enough. Their happiness underlined her own misery. Tactfully she suggested to her aunt that she might help to solve a minor domestic crisis.

166

She escorted Mrs Harcourt from the room leaving the two young people alone for a few short minutes. Mrs Harcourt wished to lie down to recover from the excitement and by the time Dorothea had got her settled Lord Sowerby had left, promising to return to escort them to an evening party later on. Clio wished to discuss the whole affair with her cousin and to talk exhaustively, first of the betrothal party and then of her wedding plans. When Dorothea escaped at last to the privacy of her own room she was too exhausted to think of her own problems. Instead she changed for the evening and tried to ignore her misery in the hope that it might go away.

The intervening days before the party were filled with an excited bustle of preparations, leaving little time to brood. Invitations had been dispatched by hand, the cook had been given lists of dishes to prepare. Extra servants were engaged for the evening and the small ballroom at the back of the house was opened, aired, and decorated festively.

After all this extended activity, most of which fell on Dorothea's shoulders for Clio was too excited to be able to concentrate on any task for more than a few minutes, the party itself was a disappointment. Dorothea had been kept so busy that when she was at last dressed and standing with her aunt, her cousin and Lord Sowerby to receive the guests she just felt exhausted. Her gown was of yellow silk falling in graceful folds from the high waist and covered with a netted tunic of silver with a tasselled fringe around the hem. This gave her an air of simplicity and elegance that contrasted well with Clio's fair loveliness since she was suitably attired in white, as befitted a young girl about to be betrothed.

Never had Dorothea felt her five years' seniority over Clio more than she did as the first guests streamed in. They had decided on a small dance that could not quite be classed as a ball, with a lavish buffet supper later in the evening. Dorothea was not sure whether she could survive the next few hours but knowing how important they must be to her cousin's happiness she pushed her own feelings to the back of her mind and concentrated on pleasing the guests.

Unable to bear a close conversation with the Earl of Rothley now that she had come to her senses and knew for certain there could never be a future for her with him, Dorothea avoided him and spent the first part of the evening chatting politely to her aunt's friends, the dowagers and chaperons, and providing partners for the less assured gentlemen.

It was inevitable that the earl should corner her at last; when he did so she knew that her colour was rising and that her knees were trembling while her reactions were those of a green girl in love and not the mature lady she knew herself to be now. However, his first words dispelled her embarrassment at confronting him and put the pair of them, briefly, back on the comfortable bantering footing they had enjoyed to date.

'Where have you been hiding, Miss Harcourt?' he asked, with a mischievous gleam in his eye. 'I nearly asked to be shown to the house-keeper's room to see if I could track you down there. You have been everywhere at once all evening.'

'Have I indeed, sir? Well I have undertaken the arrangements for my aunt to relieve her and I wanted the party to be perfect for my cousin and Lord Sowerby. It is a night to remember for them.'

'So it is. And I hope it will be for you too,' he added, and his tone was serious. Then he went on in a lighter vein. 'I hope you will now spare me the time to dance with me, Miss Harcourt. I have waited patiently for you to do your duty but I have decided to monopolize you from now on.'

Not quite sure how to take this, but guessing he was teasing her, Dorothea gave him her hand and he led her on to the floor. They made a striking couple and for a moment she was glad she had worn such an elegant gown, for he was so splendid in his superbly cut evening clothes, his hair, *à la* Brutus, in casual disorder that looked magnificent, while his cravat was enough to turn many young fops green with envy at its intricacies. She enjoyed the dance, giving herself up to the pleasure of the moment and in total accord with her partner. She almost floated around the ballroom unaware that many other guests were covertly watching them and speculating.

When the music ceased the buffet supper was served and the happy couple were toasted by all present. The earl insisted on escorting Dorothea into the meal and told her roundly that there was nothing further with which she need bother her head.

'The party is a success and you are to be envied,' he told her. 'I can see many society hostesses wishing their own gatherings were so well attended. This will rate as one of the most fashionable squeezes of the Little Season, I assure you. Now, if you have finished your supper I wish to have a few words with you. Is there anywhere where we can speak in private?'

Startled, Dorothea put down her plate, still

half-filled for she had little appetite, and nodded. He sounded so serious that she was fearful that he had already heard some scandalous rumour about her past and was about to challenge her. She was therefore quite unprepared for what he did say when they were alone in a small withdrawing room off the ballroom.

'What is it, Lord Rothley?' Dorothea asked him anxiously. He was standing silently beside a small pembroke table on which stood a silver rose-bowl filled with flowers. Their perfume filled the air and she picked nervously at a bloom, shredding petals on to the Aubusson carpet.

'Why so formal?' he countered. 'I thought we had progressed beyond such a stage. In fact I was about to ask you if I could make use of your given name,' he added.

'You were?' Dorothea was now totally puzzled.

The earl did not enlighten her immediately. Instead he changed the subject slightly. 'Have you forgiven me for deceiving you so shabbily in Derbyshire? I confess to a slight conscience on the subject.'

'Only slight, I'm sure, sir!' Dorothea teased, relieved that this was all he wanted to say. Her secret was still safe. 'Why, of course I have forgiven you. I can even see the joke myself now, although I was ashamed of my gullibility at the time. You will not take me in again.'

He smiled slightly and his dark eyes held relief. 'Good. Then I think I can now say what I wanted to you with an easier mind. Will you do me the honour of becoming my wife?'

'What did you say, sir?' Dorothea stood and gaped at him as if paralyzed. Her fingers holding the petals of one choice bloom opened and a shower of gold fell to the ground. Neither of them noticed it. '*What* did you say, Lord Rothley?'

He had been standing erect and rather stiff and now he moved forward and took her unresisting hands in his. 'I asked you to be my wife,' he repeated patiently. 'And I hope you will agree. I think we should suit admirably.'

'Your wife!' Dorothea knew the words had come out as a strangled gasp but in truth she had some difficulty in breathing and her throat was tight. She had relaxed, then suddenly he had dropped this thunderbolt on her. He was the one man in the world with whom she would care to ally herself for the rest of her days, and for that very reason — and because she cared so much — she could never do so.

Gulping back a lump that had risen in her throat she managed to say, 'You do me honour, sir, but what you propose is impossible. I must refuse you, though I thank you for your courtesy.' It was said and her breath came out in a whoosh.

Rothley frowned and his grip on her fingers tightened. 'You have not forgiven me, then. I thought you were too generous of spirit to hold such a prank against me for this long. I had no intention of causing you pain, you know. I was merely enjoying myself in a thoughtless way. It will not happen again.'

'I know — I mean — that is not the reason for my refusal, sir.' She gabbled distractedly. 'I cannot marry you and, I pray you, do not ask me why. You are very kind but it will not do. Now I must go. Please excuse me.' She tried to pull her fingers away but he held on to her.

'You may leave when you have given me a reason for your refusal,' he said firmly. 'I cannot understand why you do not even consider the advantages marriage to me must bring. I thought us friends and as my wife you could have everything you wish for. Think it over.' Unaccustomed to meeting with any refusal of his slightest whim, or indeed any kind of rebuff, the earl was genuinely incredulous. He knew his worth and any one of a dozen or so mamas would have been weeping for joy, let alone their daughters. His delight in this young woman's company, which he thought was mutual had led him to expect her to be as ecstatic as her cousin at his proposal. Even as he watched her draw herself up and stiffen he knew he had spoken arrogantly, been clumsy when he should have been adoring, and his consternation increased.

'I have said you do me great honour, sir, but I must decline your flattering offer,' Dorothea repeated with as much composure as she could muster. Her heart was thumping wildly as he held on to her fingers. He was so close that she could see the long, thick eyelashes round his dark eyes, and she longed for him to press his full, generous mouth down on hers, but it was impossible. Samantha Howard's face floated into her mind and stood between them, as it would for ever. 'If you will excuse me,' she said again as coldly as she could.

'Of course, Miss Harcourt. I am sorry to have importuned you. Your servant.' He had dropped her hands at her last words and now gave a stiff bow before moving swiftly from the room, closing the door behind him.

Dorothea sagged against the table and almost knocked the flowers to the floor. She was completely spent and could hardly see for tears, but at any moment someone might come in and see her. It would not do to give the tattle-mongers any food for gossip. She had to control her trembling knees and try to forget the amazed look on the earl's face at her refusal. Earlier he had remarked that he hoped it might be a night for her to remember, too, and this was the reason. He had intended to offer for her but she had not thought it possible until he had spoken. He must think her either a flighty female or one to bear a grudge, though neither supposition would be correct. Oh, why did she have to have a secret past that precluded any future happiness? It was so unfair. For a moment she wanted only to scream and cry out her misery, but common sense, and good manners prevailed. She had to return and entertain the guests: this was Clio's evening. Nothing must spoil it. Later she could give way but now she must control herself and go back to the ballroom.

Five minutes later she was able to do so and appear tolerably composed. Lady Garland, spying her, came rushing across and caught hold of her arm. 'Did I see you and Rothley at supper together, my dear? He has this minute left the party on the plea of another engagement but he looked very put out. Did you have words?'

If one pair of sharp eyes had noticed so would others have done. Dorothea wanted his proposal to remain a secret between the two of them, for he would be hurt and annoyed at a refusal and at the amusement this would afford the *ton*. 'Why, of course we didn't have words,' she said with a smile. 'He enjoyed the refreshments and the party. Indeed he told me it was going to be the fashionable squeeze of the Little Season. I expect he really has another engagement, you know. He is most sought after and we are lucky he came tonight. It is only because of his friendship with Lord Sowerby, but we are honoured.' She knew she had explained too much and that Lady Garland was regarding her thoughtfully, but the older woman patted her arm.

'I am sure you are right, my dear. I shall certainly say so to anyone who mentions the matter. He is right, too, it seems a most successful squeeze. You are to be congratulated. Now doesn't dear little Clio look wonderful. I am so happy for them both. An early wedding will be just the thing.' She chattered on and Dorothea had a few moments to recover her composure.

Fortunately few others seemed to have remarked the earl's early departure, although when the party was over Clio did say that

James had noticed his friend leaving.

'He had another engagement,' Dorothea explained quickly and Clio nodded. She was not interested in the Earl of Rothley's movements, only those of her beloved James.

Sowerby, in spite of or perhaps because of his own happiness, had noticed more than just the earl's early departure. He had seen the couple enter the withdrawing room, then, later, his friend come out alone looking thunderous and quite unlike his normal assured self. He had not been surprised to see him leave almost at once and he had also noted Miss Harcourt's pallor and drawn expression in the later stages of the evening.

Therefore the next day, after presenting himself in Arlington Street to thank his beloved's family for the party and to promise to take Clio up later on for a drive in the park, he repaired to his friend's large and distinguished mansion.

Shown in by the butler, Lord Sowerby was informed that my lord was breakfasting. Since it was well after noon it was easy to guess that the earl had enjoyed a late night, for whatever reason. Sowerby entered the breakfast room and greeted his friend cheerfully.

'You look somewhat the worse for wear, Detherfield,' he announced tactlessly. 'Late night at Watier's, eh? You must have lost a fortune by your expression.'

'I won,' he was told sourly. 'More than three hundred pounds and reached home soon after one of the clock, so no late night.'

'Just no sleep,' his friend remarked rather more shrewdly. 'Refused you, did she? Thought as much.'

'And you are now going to say 'I told you so'. If I remember, you did say my charm would fail with her and you have been proved correct.' Detherfield pushed his plate of ham away and got to his feet wearily.

'I'm sorry, old fellow,' Sowerby said awkwardly. 'Plenty of other girls will take you with pleasure. Miss Mayland can't wait.'

'I don't want any other girls,' the earl ground out furiously. 'I just want one brown-haired, spirited young lady who refuses to confide in me and who consistently keeps me at a distance. I'm not even sure she cares a fig for me, or otherwise surely she would have accepted me?' In his misery he was franker than he had intended to be.

Sowerby paced up and down in thought. 'She must know your worth, man,' he said at length. 'You are the greatest catch on the marriage mart. Nobody would refuse you. Stands to reason they wouldn't, with your money and looks,' he added kindly.

'I reminded her of the advantages marriage

to me would bring but she was unimpressed.' Even hours afterwards the earl was still amazed at this.

James Sowerby looked up at him. 'You talked of the advantages she would have when married to you?' he repeated incredulously. 'That don't sound like your usual polished charm, old fellow. Where were the compliments? Did you tell her you loved her?'

'Of course not,' snapped the earl irritably. 'I was proposing marriage, not enacting some romantic novel.'

Sowerby threw up his hands in despair. 'I don't wonder she refused you, then. I love my Clio and I told her so,' he added with simple honesty. 'Of course, if you don't care for Miss Harcourt except to think she would make you a good wife I do understand the difference. A few women will not marry just for position and money, though.'

'And she is one of them.'

'Must be,' Sowerby agreed. 'Oh well, try again later and she may change her mind; or if your affections are not engaged propose to another lady. You will find no lack of willing partners.'

'So you have already said,' the earl remarked with justifiable annoyance. 'I thank you for your advice.' He walked to the door and ran his hand through his disordered hair.

Sowerby suddenly noticed that his friend had no cravat on and his shirt was awry. He was in a sorry state.

'I really think I have made a mess of it, James,' Rothley murmured and thumped the door with his fist. 'Nobody has refused me anything before. What shall I do?'

'Come to White's and drown your sorrows,' Sowerby suggested promptly. 'Then try again in a week or so.'

The earl intended to follow this excellent advice in theory but did not manage it in practice. When he met Miss Harcourt again two days later he was stiff and awkward with her and their old comradeship had gone. She did her best to avoid him and spoke to him as little as possible. He was afraid she found him distant and he certainly thought her cold.

Dorothea was extremely miserable. She kept up a pretence of happiness for the sake of her aunt and Clio which made her physically unwell. She grew paler and within a week was feeling listless and depressed and longing for the time when they could retire to Bedfordshire. Her only relief was that the earl's proposal still remained a secret between them. She had not confided in Clio or her aunt, although she guessed, from his sympathetic expression, that Lord Sowerby knew what had occurred. But society in general was unaware of it. Speculation began again that the earl intended to offer for Miss Mayland when he escorted her to the theatre and Dorothea felt more miserable than ever. She had a crumb of comfort in that Mrs Howard did not know of the earl's proposal, but as Mr Arnold could find out no more about the lady the future looked bleak indeed.

A fortnight after the party Dorothea went into her cousin's chamber just after five o'clock, intending to ask what Clio would wear for a forthcoming musical evening. She found Annie in a state of collapse and the room in total disorder.

'Why, whatever has happened, Annie?' she asked in surprise. 'Has my cousin gone mad, to be throwing her clothes all around, and why are you crying like that? Come, girl, what is amiss?' she added more sharply as Annie's sobs increased in volume.

'Oh, Miss Dorothea, Miss Dorothea, she's gone!' wailed Annie. 'She's gone and I dunno what to do.'

'Stop crying and tell me what you mean at once,' Dorothea commanded. 'Who has gone? Surely not Clio?'

Annie nodded and mopped her streaming eyes on her apron. 'Oh yes, she has,' she gulped in distress. 'She has gone and it's all my fault.' A fresh wail followed. Dorothea crossed the room and slapped her heartily.

'Stop that and tell me what you mean.'

Dazed but suddenly quiet, Annie gulped again and got out, 'I was up here with Miss Clio, choosing her gown. She got a message from the footman — Bert it was — that a young gentleman wanted her downstairs. She thought it was Lord Sowerby and dashed off and I never saw her again.'

Tears seemed imminent once more but Dorothea was not having that. 'Where did she go? Why is this place in such a mess? Explain to me, Annie. Now,' she added impatiently.

'I dunno where she's gone but another lady come up here a few minutes later and demanded some clothes to be packed in a bandbox. I did as she said because she told me Miss Clio would suffer otherwise. It was that lady we seen in Matlock,' Annie added. Her grammar had gone to pieces in her distress.

Even as the maid was speaking Dorothea had grown cold with fear. Now she elicited a description of the lady who had come to the bedchamber; it was indeed Mrs Howard. It could be no other. But where had Clio gone? Annie did not know and the lady had not said. The maid was sure of that. However the lady had left a note to be given to Miss

Dorothea no earlier than six of the clock, or Miss Clio would suffer.

It was now just after five and Dorothea demanded it at once. There was little to be gained from the intelligence for the lines read: *I have decided to combine plans one and two since Martin Detherfield is now looking elsewhere. If you value your cousin then find £500 pounds in gold and be prepared to deliver it wherever you are instructed.* That was all.

For a moment Dorothea was stunned by the enormous cheek of the woman. Then she wondered why on earth Clio had gone with them, particularly since she was betrothed. How had the wretched Mr Simmonds persuaded her, for he must have been the young man waiting below? It was a mystery but Dorothea foresaw worse than the loss of £500 in gold. If Clio was not recovered that evening her reputation would be ruined, and Simmonds would have to marry her because nobody else would. Lord Sowerby would never believe that she had merely accompanied a man and woman in a coach. He loved her, but he would not want compromised goods. It was a dreadful tangle. How on earth was she to find Clio in a few hours and keep the whole matter secret?

9

Her first task was to reassure her aunt. She went at once to that lady and told her a little of what had taken place, but she pretended that Clio had gone to help Mrs Howard and that she, Dorothea, was going after her as chaperon. Mrs Harcourt was naturally upset but she trusted her niece and promised to say nothing to anyone. Annie was sworn to silence and detailed to accompany Dorothea. The old barouche was brought round to the door and the two women got in. Dorothea had also interrogated the footman, Bert, who had taken up the original message. He could give her little information beyond confirming that it had been Mr Simmonds, from her description of the man. However, when the hackney had stopped in front of the house the second time to pick up the fine lady — Mrs Howard — he had overheard the young man telling the coachman to make haste to Uxbridge. He rather thought Miss Clio was already in the coach by then, but he had not seen her so could not be certain.

With only this rather muddling information to go on Dorothea knew her pursuit was likely to be doomed to failure, but she had to make the attempt. She tucked all the money she possessed in the house, a mere hundred pounds, into her reticule and gave the coachman instructions to take the road to Uxbridge.

Even as the vehicle began to move Dorothea started to worry. What could she do on her own, a mere female, against two such opponents as Mrs Howard and Mr Simmonds? Clio, after being abducted, was unlikely to be of much help and Annie had already begun to sniffle again. Without stopping to think of the propriety of her action or even consider their present strained relations she stopped the coach and gave directions to the Earl of Rothley's town house. She dared not inform Lord Sowerby, for he must be kept in ignorance, but the earl was powerful and could advise her what to do when she caught up with the runaways.

She was so desperate that, trailing Annie behind her, she swept past the astonished butler and demanded to see the earl immediately.

'My lord is dressing for dinner,' the butler objected, affronted. He could see that this lady had style and recognized the name she gave him, but he would not interrupt his master. 'I cannot disturb his lordship at the moment,' he went on loftily. 'You may wait in the withdrawing room if you wish.'

'I have no time for that. I will have to go up and see him myself,' Dorothea said with grim determination.

'But ma'am, you cannot,' the butler cried out, scandalized.

Dorothea had already got her foot on the bottom step of the impressive staircase. 'Unless you tell his lordship that I am here and desire to see him at once on a matter of extreme urgency I will go up,' she said icily.

Acknowledging defeat, the butler made a stately progress up the stairs after ushering the two women into the withdrawing room on the ground floor. Annie was totally overawed by the house and her mistress's sudden outrageous behaviour, and was still upset over Miss Clio's disappearance. She hovered near the fireplace sniffling and clutching her shabby cloak around her while Dorothea paced up and down impatiently.

It seemed an age but it was not many minutes before the door was flung open and the Earl of Rothley strode into the room. He paused on the threshold and surveyed the two women in surprise. 'I did not believe Homes when he told me you were waiting to see me on a pressing matter but I see he was correct.' He noticed Dorothea's pallor, her agitation, and took in the crying Annie in the background. 'Well, I am glad you have not come here unescorted, but tell me at once, what can I do to help you?'

Dorothea was so relieved to see him and had such confidence in his judgement that as soon as she heard this sympathetic remark she poured out the whole story. She pulled Mrs Howard's terse note from her reticule and handed it to the earl. 'I thought I must set out after them immediately, sir,' she said quickly. 'I cannot tell my aunt the whole so I came to you for advice. What must I do when I catch up with them? You see . . . ' For a moment only she hesitated. 'You see, this Mrs Howard is blackmailing me and I fear she will stop at nothing to gain her ends. Also you saw how besotted the wretched Mr Simmonds is with my cousin. I fear for her.'

The earl had been thinking deeply, and a frown creased his brow. He moved to the door and called out, 'Get Sharpe to bring round my carriage and the bays and quickly.' He turned back to Dorothea and smiled at her warmly. 'Don't worry. We will soon catch up with them for a hired hackney is no match for my lightweight carriage and the fastest pair in town. I will just dash off a note to James, for in spite of your fears he must know of this, but we cannot wait to collect him. I will be with you directly.'

He had gone before Dorothea could gather her thoughts, but she felt enormous relief that the matter was out of her hands. If he accompanied her then Mrs Howard would be vanquished. She had complete faith in him. Hard on this came the knowledge that he had not taken any notice of her mention of blackmail nor had he seemed surprised. Perhaps he had not heard her and she would have to explain later. Even this gloomy thought did not spoil her gratitude and relief.

The earl was back in an incredibly short time, changed from his evening attire into buckskins and a blue coat with a travelling cape on his arm. 'The carriage is here,' he told the women. 'I have instructed your coachman to return to Arlington Street, but we will take your maid with us to preserve your reputation.' His tone was perfectly serious as he led the way out of the house and Dorothea followed, pulling the reluctant Annie after her.

She and the maid were settled inside the coach but the earl leapt up to the driving seat and set the horses in motion. Not sorry to have a chance to think over all that had happened Dorothea relaxed in the well-sprung comfort and tried to cheer Annie. 'Now that we have the earl's assistance I am sure we can bring Clio back with us tonight,' she said, trying to sound optimistic. 'They were not expecting us to set out after them so soon — if at all. It is not yet six of the clock, the time you were supposed to deliver the note. At what hour did you say Mrs Howard went off with Miss Clio's bags?' She wanted to reassure herself that they were not far behind their quarry.

' 'Bout half an hour before you come in and found me, Miss Dorothea,' Annie explained again patiently. She had already said the same to the earl minutes before.

'Then they have not much of a start on us and will not know that we have their direction. Thank goodness Bert has sharp ears and heard what was said. Otherwise we would never have found them.'

'Bert's very handy, miss. He's bright too, and hopes to train as under-butler in a year or two,' Annie told her proudly.

Dorothea saw the fatuous smile on the girl's face. Here was another of her household in love and likely to be able to make a match of it. Thinking of the handsome man driving them along at that moment Dorothea sighed wistfully. She might have to tell him her mother's secret and so this would be the last time she spoke to him, but if Clio was saved for Lord Sowerby her sacrifice would be worth it. One of them deserved to be happy, at least. She put aside her own dreaming and questioned Annie about her Bert, glad that their faithful maid had found an admirer amongst the London servants hired with the house.

The carriage drew into an inn in the village of Acton for the earl to enquire about passing travellers. He gained no information from the surly landlord of the rather shabby inn and they were soon on their way again, being driven fast across Ealing Common. Dorothea twisted her hands together nervously in her lap as the miles sped by. Would they catch up with her cousin and her scheming captors or had they chosen a different route? What would Clio's fate be if they did not succeed in finding her? This was even more frightening and did not bear thinking about.

It was quite dark when they reached Uxbridge. Neither of the women had any idea of how long they had been on the road but it was a relief to see the lights of the houses ahead. At the first inn the earl drew a blank but at the next inn, a larger place with more rooms, his questions were successful. The hackney was still in the yard, the driver was in the taproom and the passengers were in a private parlour, having a meal, so the landlord informed him.

The earl dealt with the driver and a suitably large bribe changed hands so that the man was quite willing to leave his unfinished ale and go back to London. 'For I had no idea they was abducting your ward, guv, my lord I mean,' he added and disappeared before he could be blamed for anything.

Dorothea, with Annie still behind her but looking less miserable and more excited now that they were in reach of her mistress, were ushered into an adjoining parlour. The earl closed the door behind the landlord after sending for refreshments.

'We must go in and rescue Clio at once, sir,' Dorothea cried. 'We cannot be waiting around for food and drink. I thought you would help me.'

'So I have and so I will. Don't fret,' he told her soothingly. 'The last thing you want, surely, is to arouse the landlord's suspicions and create the very scandal we wish to avoid. Therefore we order refreshments as expected. I have told him we will probably join our friends later but he is not to say anything, for we wish to surprise them. In this way I discovered the exact room they are in. As soon as the food is brought we may discreetly force Mrs Howard to give up your cousin.'

'I wish we may do so, sir.' Dorothea shivered. 'She is so unpleasant and . . . and . . . '

She floundered to a stop, not wanting to repeat what she had said earlier but knowing she must do so.

'I know,' he told her firmly. 'She has threatened you, but then she did not expect to have me to deal with, did she? I think I am more than a match for any Mrs Howard, however vulgar she may be,' he added lightly.

Dorothea managed a weak smile but she was too anxious about the delay. She wished the landlord would hurry and bring the meal they had ordered. Her companion chatted pleasantly while they waited and Annie brightened sufficiently to reply once or twice when her mistress remained silent and preoccupied.

At last the landlord bustled in, followed by two maids to lay the table and serve the dishes, such was the earl's consequence. The good man recognized the Quality when he saw it, he also remembered the largesse that the earl had distributed. The food smelled delicious but Dorothea was too worried to eat. When they were again alone the earl took pity on her and, instructing Annie to make a good meal in their absence, he took the young woman's arm. He led her out and down the corridor to the neighbouring parlour.

It was possible to hear Mrs Howard's

strident tones coming through the wooden door; there seemed to be an altercation in progress between her and her nephew. Dorothea's fear and nervousness increased and she faltered, looking beseechingly up at the earl. He gave her an encouraging smile, opened the door and strode confidently into the room.

Beside him Dorothea found her courage and followed him, closing the door behind her in case anyone should overhear them. She gazed quickly round the room, searching for Clio, and saw with relief that her cousin was reclining on a couch in one corner of the room and weeping into an already sodden handkerchief. She rushed across to clasp the girl in her arms. When Clio saw who had arrived she burst into loud wails and threw herself at Dorothea.

'Oh, she says I must marry him but I can't — I can't. I love James. Oh help me, Dottie. Take me home with you. Please,' beseeched Clio when she could speak again coherently. She clung to her cousin, who sat down beside her and tried to soothe and calm her. The earl, meanwhile, surveyed the other two occupants of the room who had both risen in shocked surprise at their entrance.

Mrs Howard bristled with rage when she recognized them and took in exactly who they were. She was once again dressed in purple silk, her favourite colour and material, and wore what looked like a diamond necklace around her throat. Her yellow curls bobbed in indignation and her bosom swelled. 'How dare you come into this room. This is a private parlour and I will have you thrown out at once.'

'How dare you abduct my cousin,' Dorothea shouted back from the couch. She had found her courage again now that she was reunited with Clio, who was still unharmed.

Before Mrs Howard could reply the earl said quietly, 'Hardly an abduction, more a theatrical farce.' His cool tones dampened Dorothea's fury, and indeed Mrs Howard's expression was comical. Her mouth opened and she stared at him in amazement. 'Have you anything further to say before I tell you what I am going to do?' the earl went on, raising an enquiring eyebrow.

'I most certainly have,' the widow exploded. 'Tom, what are you thinking of? Do something at once. The young lady is your responsibility, after all.'

The wretched youth flushed, stammered and tried to utter something, but found his neckcloth suddenly too tight as the earl subjected him to a long scrutiny. 'I . . . I . . . Clio and I are to be married,' he got out in a rush.

Mrs Howard smiled and shot a look of triumph at Dorothea. Clio wailed again and buried her face in her hands. The earl merely opened his snuff box and took a delicate pinch before speaking.

'I believe Lord Sowerby, Miss Harcourt's betrothed, is only moments behind us on the road. I am sure he can clear up any misunderstandings with you on that score. I think he could make a nice mess of your face and figure. Perhaps scar you for life. He will certainly be in a murderous mood, I imagine.'

His words and his casual actions completely cowed the red-faced Simmonds, who collapsed on his chair and clutched at his hair. 'I cannot. I will not fight,' he stuttered, then he gazed accusingly at Mrs Howard. 'I told you it would never work, Aunt. It was a foolish plan from the start.'

'I do so agree with you,' the earl murmured smoothly. He sat himself on the edge of the table and swung one gleaming hessian boot idly to and fro. Simmonds buried his face in his hands and looked as if he wished he could dissolve into unmanly tears too. Mrs Howard was far stronger; she at once took a step towards the earl and raised her finger threateningly.

'Oh no, my lord. You will not find me so easy to subdue as all that. Maybe taking that girl was a mistake, since she has done nothing but blubber for hours now and I am heartily sick of her. However, you cannot just walk in and remove her like that. You ask her,' she added, pointing at Dorothea. 'She knows what I mean.'

'Oh so do I, so do I,' the earl said softly, but there was menace in his tone now. 'You are a common blackmailer, are you not, Mrs Howard? Also, you are even worse than that for you are a thief and I can prove it. I had a mind to lay the case before the magistrates a while back when I first heard Miss Harcourt's tale but I thought I would await developments. Now I shall have no such scruples.'

The older woman's highly coloured face went pale, leaving her paint standing out in garish spots. 'So you know the story,' she said huskily. 'I never thought she would tell you. She was too ashamed. So that must be why you are no longer dangling after her.' She gave Dorothea a look of vicious hatred and subsided into her chair in a flurry of purple skirts.

'I do not intend to explain anything to you, madam,' the earl snapped. A dangerous light gleamed in his dark eyes. 'You will control your impudent tongue, however, unless you wish to spend all your remaining days in a Newgate cell.'

'You can't threaten me,' blustered Mrs Howard. 'I have done nothing wrong. Nothing at all and I will still spread the scandal in society. Those two will be ruined, for Lord Sowerby will not marry her when he hears whom she is related to, any more than you wanted her cousin.'

The earl took a pace forward. The fury in his expression made even Mrs Howard shrink. With one hand he ripped off her diamond necklace and dangled it from his long, white fingers as she shrieked in alarm. 'Oh yes, I think Newgate for you anyway. This will condemn you if nothing else does, Sarah Simmonds.'

Samantha Howard shrank further back and grew even paler. Her hands clutched her throat which now showed a red weal and she mumbled, 'I don't know what you mean.'

'Oh, I think you do. I have had you thoroughly investigated. You were once a maid to Melissa DeVine, were you not? You stole a quantity of jewellery from her and absconded from her service some five years ago, leaving a letter threatening exposure of the daughter whom, she confided to you, she had left in England years before. Knowing you to be unscrupulous she did not seek you out to reclaim her property, some fifty thousand pounds worth of jewels, I believe.

197

Now do you know what I mean?'

Dorothea and Clio were both sitting upright, staring in fascination at the scene. Tom Simmonds had lifted his head and was also gazing at his aunt in amazement. Then he stared at the necklace which was still in the earl's fingers.

'Nonsense. It's all nonsense,' Mrs Howard got out at last. A little colour returned to her cheeks as she pointed at the necklace. 'Take that to any jeweller, my lord, and ask him. He will tell you that those gems are paste. I like pretty things but I cannot afford them. I am no thief.'

'I have already been to several jewellers and discovered where you had the originals copied and where you sold them for a fraction of their real value. I think I can prove my case against you in any law court, and I will do so if you force me to.' He broke the necklace into three pieces and threw them on the floor contemptuously. Mrs Howard wailed in horror as she watched and Dorothea marvelled at the strength in his lean fingers.

'Now,' continued the earl, 'I hope you will see sense and change your mind about repeating scandalous tales which would do a great deal of unnecessary harm and cause suffering to innocent people, apart from staining the name of a lady now dead who cannot defend herself. She was also most generous to you, I think,' he added.

Mrs Howard sniffed and muttered then looked sullenly at the earl. 'And if I don't keep quiet? What then?' she demanded.

'You will go to gaol for an unspecified length of time. My word is always taken and I know most of the judges well. You cannot escape by lying to any of them.'

She scowled furiously. 'Very well then. I will keep the secret, though much good may that do her since you know all about it anyway.' She glared venomously at Dorothea, clearly blaming her for all that had just taken place. 'But I have a price, sir. I will accept two thousand pounds to keep quiet, and cheap at that. You can afford it,' she added rashly.

'Oh indeed I can, but I don't intend to give you anything. You are an insolent, scheming hussy. Perhaps we had better discuss the fraudulent sale you made of a certain sapphire pendant which still adorns the neck of a reigning fashionable lady. We both know it to be paste, do we not? I wonder how she would react if she knew also? Ah, I see you do not wish to put my speculation to the test. Very sensible. I suggest you take yourself and this object whom you call nephew off as fast as possible and don't show your face in society again. Remember I have a long arm and retribution is cheap for me, if you should ever be tempted to talk rashly. Now get out. I think I hear a coach outside, which is probably Lord Sowerby's. I suggest you leave by the kitchen door,' he shouted as Simmonds grabbed his hat and scuttled desperately to escape.

Mrs Howard picked up her pelisse, her reticule and her muff. With a furious glance at the two women on the couch she stalked from the room as quickly as she could without losing all her dignity.

'Now, let us repair to our own parlour to await James's arrival,' the earl murmured. 'I expect I will have to settle the bill for this room too, as they will not have paid the shot.' He sighed as he got off the table and studied the littered remains of the meal. 'Come along,' he added. He opened the door courteously.

Dorothea pulled Clio to her feet and both of them moved into the passage. Dorothea walked into their own parlour and Annie jumped up as a flurry of booted feet was heard on the steps.

'Where is she? Where have the wretches taken her? I'll murder the lot of them,' roared Sowerby as he came into view.

With a glad cry Clio threw herself into his

arms and began to sob and stutter out her story.

The earl bundled them both unceremoniously into the parlour that they had just vacated. 'Miss Harcourt will tell you everything, James, but do not be informing the entire hostelry of your affairs,' he said firmly as he closed the door on them. 'And now we can have our dinner in peace,' he added as he joined Dorothea and Annie.

The maid had just been reassured that Clio was safe. She bobbed a quick curtsey and murmured, 'I will just be going down to the landlord to ask him to send up another hot pie.' She disappeared out of the door.

'What a good girl,' Rothley said approvingly and sat down after Dorothea had seated herself rather abruptly.

Now that the confrontation was all over and Clio was safe she found she was trembling. Her legs would hardly support her. Reaction had set in and she shivered at the thought of Mrs Howard's venom and frustrated fury. Her mind was still trying to take in all she had heard, including the startling revelations made by the earl. How he had found all this out she had no idea but to turn the tables on the woman as he had done was masterly. Even in her weakened state she could appreciate all he had said and how he had reduced the opposition to nothing.

Thoughtfully the earl poured out a glass of wine and handed it to her. 'Drink this and you will feel better,' he encouraged her. 'The last few minutes have been unpleasant for us all, but necessary in order to squash her pretensions. I don't think you need worry that she will trouble you any further. She is by far too frightened of what I know of her activities.' He sipped at a glass he had poured for himself and smiled at her kindly.

Feeling better as the wine warmed her Dorothea began to think. 'How did you find out so much, Lord Rothley?' she asked. 'Mr Arnold, my lawyer, could find no traces of Mrs Howard, let alone her past. I was amazed when you talked to her. Is she really a thief?'

'Oh yes,' he told her calmly. 'She worked for your mother for two years, wormed her way into her confidence and as your mother grew frail when she was bereaved and weaker in health the woman began to steal her jewellery. Eventually greed overcame any scruples she had and she took more, then absconded, leaving a threatening note behind. She has been living on the proceeds of that theft ever since.'

He seemed to know all about her mother so Dorothea made no comment on the first part of what he had said. So much still needed explaining. 'How did you know she was once Sarah Simmonds?'

'Ah well, one of my investigators found an accomplice of this Sarah's and, as Sarah's description tallied with that of Mrs Howard, he delved deeper and found them to be one and the same. It was a lucky chance, but she had become overconfident as all thieves do.'

'I am so grateful to, you, sir, for helping me,' Dorothea murmured, suddenly overcome by all that they owed to this man. 'If you had not brought us here so fast they could have been gone and I dread to think how I would have managed alone.'

'I was glad to help, although I was surprised that you came to me at all, in view of how distant you have been for some days now. But may I hope you are not now so unfriendly as you were?'

'No, of course not, sir. I have not been distant — well, not really, but it was awkward after I had refused your offer. You see . . . my mother . . . ' She floundered to a stop and for once he did not help her. He just studied her face seriously and waited for her to go on.

Before she could do so the door burst open again and Lord Sowerby, with Clio clinging to his arm, erupted into the room, demanding to be told exactly what had happened. Between explanations from the earl, who carefully omitted details of her mother's past, Dorothea noticed, and Clio's tearful story of how she had been persuaded to accompany them, no further private conversation was possible.

Dorothea was not entirely sorry that she had time to collect her wits. She was under a great obligation to the Earl of Rothley; they all were, but she did not know how to thank him properly. She was glad when Annie arrived with more hot food and they all made an excellent dinner in relief at being safe at last.

James Sowerby summed up their feelings as he placed an arm around his beloved. 'To think that none of this would have happened if my little Clio had not cared for me so much. To risk herself rushing to my aid, as she thought, when she had been told a lying tale. I am the luckiest man alive that the matter is settled satisfactorily and no harm done. All is well now and nobody need know of it.'

10

After the meal, all three women were very tired from the excitements of the evening. It was only ten o'clock but it seemed much later to them and both men decided that it would be safer to drive home at once, particularly as Mrs Harcourt would be worried by now about her daughter and niece and there was no way of putting her mind at rest unless they returned. Clio refused to be parted from Lord Sowerby, so he took her down to his curricle and sat her up beside him, well wrapped in travelling rugs. She was completely happy now that she was safe and back with her beloved James, yet she remained unaware of how great had been her danger. To her cousin's relief she also appeared ignorant of the true story behind Mrs Howard's abduction of her and the threats the lady had used.

Dorothea and Annie were put inside the earl's comfortable carriage and he once more took the reins. Although free from the fear of exposure for the first time for months, Dorothea was not really happy as they drove back to London. She wondered how the earl had found out so much and what he really thought of her and her sordid past. He had discovered the whole truth and she was inclined to believe that Mrs Howard was right: that his recent coolness toward her was in consequence of this knowledge. She was not surprised but she was hurt.

It was very hard to be ostracized for no fault of her own, but only an accident of birth, although she did not blame him for his reactions. In his position only the best would do and he could pick and choose a wife anywhere. She had, after all, refused him before he found out the truth so that when he did know her background it was natural that he would have a disgust of her. She was very grateful that he had kept her secret to himself and also that he had been good enough to come with her and help her rescue her cousin. At least she was now free of Mrs Howard's importunities and could look to the future. But without the Earl of Rothley it held little of interest to her.

When they drew nearer to Arlington Street her dejection grew more pronounced, partly because of her exhausted state. She was thankful to be back when the carriage drew up in front of the house but could only manage a polite expression of her gratitude to the earl as he escorted her to the door.

'I am really grateful, Lord Rothley,' she told him. 'I know I would never have succeeded in bringing my cousin home and of freeing myself from Mrs Howard without your assistance. I am deeply in your debt.'

He took her hand and bowed over it formally. 'The pleasure was mine, Miss Harcourt. I was glad to be of service. If you will permit me I will call tomorrow to see how you all do after this eventful evening. Your servant.' He bowed again and left her and Annie just as the butler opened the door to usher them inside.

There followed another trying hour before Dorothea could escape to the sanctuary of her bedchamber. Mrs Harcourt had retired, but was sitting up in her bed awaiting their return with great concern. Dorothea went in to her aunt and explained as much of what had happened as she thought necessary. She was soon interrupted by Clio when she reached home. With all the tears, the recital of events yet again and the nervous strain, by the time Dorothea climbed between the sheets in the peace of her own room she had a bad headache. This persisted and next morning she felt unequal to getting up at all. She was still very downcast when she thought of her own future and compared it with that of Clio. Mrs Howard's words concerning the earl ceasing his attentions to her when he learned the truth of her background had gone through her head repeatedly all night. When Clio came in looking radiant and asked after her, Dorothea turned her face to the wall and admitted to feeling unwell.

She did indeed seem to have a feverish turn and Mrs Harcourt, who followed her daughter to see the invalid, insisted she stay where she was because she must have caught a chill the evening before. Dorothea was glad to remain in the quiet of her room, for she had no wish to see the Earl of Rothley if he should indeed call as he had promised. Yet later, when Clio reported that he had called to ask after her she was irrationally disappointed that she had not been downstairs to talk to him.

She remained in her room for two days. When she was fully recovered she joined her aunt in the withdrawing room to sew listlessly throughout the next day, when the earl did not make an appearance. Clio and her aunt went out to a party that night but Dorothea refused to attend. All she longed to do was return to Bedfordshire, and she wondered how soon she could suggest they should go back there to make the necessary wedding preparations for Clio's nuptials in mid-December.

On the fourth day after the dramatic drive to Uxbridge, when Dorothea was sitting alone in the drawing room, again attempting to sew, she was amazed when the earl was shown in. She got to her feet and colour stained her pale cheeks. 'Oh, sir, my aunt has just this minute gone out. She and my cousin are gone shopping to Bond Street. You have just missed them.'

'I did not come to see Mrs Harcourt nor your cousin but to ask after you,' the earl replied gravely as he bowed over her hand. His dark eyes searched her face and he frowned. 'I am afraid you are still unwell. Please sit down and I will not keep you long. I just called to enquire how you are going along.'

'Oh I am perfectly fit, sir,' Dorothea said with a sigh. 'It is kind of you to ask.'

He sat beside her and placed his hands on the knees of his beige-coloured pantaloons. 'What is wrong?' he asked bluntly. 'You are not yourself and if you are not ill then what is the matter? Please tell me.'

He sounded genuinely concerned and Dorothea responded without thinking. 'I wish I could leave London and return to Bedfordshire,' she explained sadly. 'I believe I am grown weary of society. The shallowness and stupidity of fashionable life has lost its appeal.'

'I see,' he said thoughtfully. 'You have no need to worry that anyone will learn your secret from me, you know, Miss Harcourt. I have told no one what I discovered, not even James. Your cousin, too, is still in ignorance so you may be comfortable on that score.'

'You are very kind,' she murmured.

He got to his feet abruptly. 'I think you need some fresh air to blow away your low spirits. Come, Miss Harcourt, let me take you for a drive. We shall visit in Kensington and you will feel much better.'

Torn between a desire to go with him and enjoy his company even for a short while and the listlessness that had grown on her in the past few days Dorothea hesitated.

'Come. You will not disappoint an old lady who has been looking forward to meeting you these last three days.'

'Who is it, sir?' Dorothea asked him, curious in spite of herself.

'My grandmother, Lady Rothley. She is a marvellous lady and I have spoken of you to her. She is hoping to meet you and I know you will like each other. Come and see her to please me.'

It was impossible to refuse such a request and in truth Dorothea suddenly found she was tired of the house in Arlington Street. A drive with the earl would lift her spirits. She got to her feet with a smile and nodded her head. 'I will come, sir. I think you are right and the fresh air will do me good. I will go and fetch my pelisse if you will but wait a moment. Shall I bring Annie?' she added as an afterthought.

'There is no need. It is not a long drive and we will return this afternoon. I have only brought my curricle, so there is no room for her,' he explained with an engaging grin. 'Do wrap up warmly, Miss Harcourt. I do not wish you to catch another chill.'

Guessing that he was teasing her she smiled back at him and tripped up to her room, feeling lighter in heart than she had done for days. He was waiting in the hall when she came downstairs some ten minutes later and in no time they were bowling along in the direction of the village of Kensington.

For a while neither of them spoke at all. Dorothea was glad just to be in his company and was feeling better for the fresh November air. The earl was wondering how to begin what he wanted to say and finding himself at a loss for words, as he had been on several occasions with this young woman.

After a few moments of companionable silence Dorothea asked him, 'Why did you tell your grandmother about me?'

In one way this gave the earl the opening

he was seeking, but in another he had no wish as yet to give her a truthful answer to this question in case she was upset. He was a direct man, though, and could not deceive her again. 'I went to my grandmother for information when I first thought you were in trouble, Miss Harcourt,' he said slowly. 'After our first drive in the park. When I saw your reaction to the chance encounter with Mrs Howard. I was surprised and decided to investigate.'

'Oh.' Dorothea was not sure what to think. She wished her companion had not been so sharp-witted and shrewd on that occasion, but maybe it had been a good thing.

'My grandmother knows everybody's family history to the year dot and I knew she could tell me something of your background if I went and asked her. She has a phenomenal memory.'

'So you thought I was some kind of impostor in society. Is that it?' she challenged him.

He sighed. There was nothing for it but to explain his conversation with James Sowerby and their deductions. When he had finished she remained silent for a moment.

'What did your grandmother tell you?'

'She remembered your mother Melissa and how she ran off with some young sprig because she could not bear her cold-hearted husband. I am sorry,' he added. 'I have no wish to distress you.'

'I have very little recollection of my parents. Of my mother I remember nothing, and of my father not much more. He visited occasionally when he was home on leave but only for a few days at a time,' Dorothea admitted honestly. 'Aunt Sophie and Uncle Edward were my parents in my eyes. I loved them like a mother and father.'

'Hearing that relieves my mind. I was concerned you might have the vapours or shriek with horror at the insult to your name if I told you the facts.'

'Surely you must know I am not that type of female.' Dorothea could not help smiling at the idea of her having the vapours.

'No, I didn't think it of you really,' he said with an engaging sideways grin. 'Well, my grandmother told me the story with embellishments produced by the passage of time. She also told me of the rumours that your mother had fallen in love with and remained the mistress of a German prince until his death. Her own demise occurred soon after. Is that correct?'

'So the lawyer said,' Dorothea agreed cautiously.

'Well, I have already told you that luck

favoured us with Mrs Howard. My man followed her and the lad and traced them to their lodgings. Further investigations revealed who she really was and what she had done. The theft of the jewellery and the copying of it was an idea that came to me when I remembered her overdressed appearance, but the beauty of the jewels was remarkable and did not go with her personality. Influence in the right quarter helped and I learned the truth.'

'Does your grandmother know the whole story?' Dorothea enquired nervously. The thought of some frightening old dowager knowing the details of Mrs Howard's career and her blackmail was too awful.

The earl patted her hand. 'No. She only knows who you are and of my interest. That is all. We have arrived at her house now.'

They had reached Kensington while they had been talking. The earl drew the curricle to a halt in front of an elegant house, rather small, but of excellent proportions. They were met by a stately butler who took them to a salon on the ground floor at the back of the house which overlooked a lovely garden. There Dorothea made her curtsey to Lady Rothley and when she saw the small, slight but very bright-eyed old lady in her upright brocade chair she relaxed a little. The earl's grandmother was like an inquisitive bird whose sharp dark eyes, so like those of Martin Detherfield, noticed everything.

'Come and sit beside me and tell me all about yourself,' Lady Rothley invited, indicating a footstool near her chair. 'Maud can entertain me grandson. Rothley's used to her be now. So you are Melissa's daughter. You look like her around the eyes but there is more character in your face, m'dear, and less beauty.'

'Grandmother, don't bully her,' the earl admonished from his seat beside a nondescript cousin, companion to the old lady, and the one referred to as Maud.

'As if I would,' the old lady cackled and proceeded to chatter away to the girl at her side, learning a great deal in a very short time. Dorothea enjoyed their talk and found Lady Rothley amusing. She had the same sense of the absurd that her grandson enjoyed and she was soon laughing happily and feeling better than she had for days. Her eyes did stray to where the earl sat patiently holding wool for Maud but she tried not to watch him too closely and not to think of what might have been.

After half an hour the old lady turned abruptly to the earl and remarked outrageously, 'Well, when are you two going to make a match of it, then?'

Dorothea blushed scarlet and the earl looked most embarrassed. His grandmother chuckled with unholy laughter and picked up her stick to poke him in the ribs. 'Haven't you asked her yet? Young sprigs were not so slow in my day. Don't look so shocked, Maud, I could tell you a tale or two.'

'Grandmother!' Rothley got to his feet and scowled rather like a naughty small boy caught stealing apples. 'I wish you would not embarrass Miss Harcourt.'

'Embarrass her? Fiddlesticks! The gal's pining for you to make an offer. Take her into the garden and talk to her while I have a nap. Then you can come in for a nuncheon before you go. Get on with it, boy,' she added, waving her stick again with happy glee.

Stiffly the earl crossed the room looking rather red in the face himself. He stopped in front of Dorothea and offered her his arm. 'Will you take a walk, Miss Harcourt?' he suggested formally. 'We have little choice.' He darted a glance of irritation at his grand-mother but she was unrepentant.

'Go on, boy,' she told him. 'Stop shilly-shallying. Use her name too. It's pretty. I like it. Come back with good news in half an hour.' She waved them off through the long glass doors that opened on to the terrace. The earl escorted the girl carefully into the garden and they walked over the grass away from the house.

'I hope you will forgive her,' he excused his relative unhappily. 'She says exactly what she thinks and will not be hushed, but she is a dear really.'

'She is a marvellous old lady,' Dorothea replied warmly. 'I can see why you are fond of her. She wanted an excuse to have a little sleep, I expect.'

'I'm not so sure of that,' he muttered sourly. 'She is an interfering old busybody when she can get away with it.'

'Only because she cares for you and has your interests at heart.'

'Well, I had no wish to have her do my proposing for me. It plays the very devil with a fellow's self-confidence,' he retorted, then lapsed into silence.

They walked on round a corner into a small rose-garden. A convenient seat was placed in the centre and the earl led Dorothea to this and indicated that she should sit down. 'Will you give me an honest answer to a question?' he asked seriously.

'Of course. Why should I do otherwise?'

He shrugged unhappily. 'You might not care to tell me the truth. I have been less than honest with you on occasion.'

'Oh fie on you. Shame!' she said cheerfully. 'I thought we agreed to forget all about that deception.'

'So we did.' He smiled too but then fidgeted with his waistcoat as if nervous. 'When you refused the offer of marriage I made to you did you do so on account of that woman's blackmail?' he asked bluntly.

Startled, Dorothea grew rosy in the face again. 'Well, yes I did,' she admitted, refusing to meet his eyes now. 'How could I accept you when she had promised to spread the story unless I found her a rich husband, which she said would be easy for me as your wife? I could not expect you to endure such blackmail nor want a wife with such a scandalous past.' She hung her head.

'It's not your past,' he said gently and lifted her chin with one hand so that she had to face him. 'Your mother's follies have been forgotten by all but my nosy old grand-mother.'

'Yet society would revel in the story if it were told,' Dorothea insisted.

'Possibly. As a seven-day wonder. But nobody will tell society for it is forgotten, as I've just said. So you did not refuse me because you have a disgust of me over our first encounters?' His confidence was growing now after her first answer.

'No, indeed, I did not have a disgust of you sir,' she whispered.

'Dare I ask if you liked me?'

'I would hardly accept invitations to drive out with you if I did not,' she returned with some spirit. He laughed in delight.

'My grandmother was quite right. We shall suit admirably. I am going to risk a second snub and ask you, Dorothea, if you will do me the honour of marrying me. Please forget all the silly nonsense about your mother's past. I care nothing for such a story for she was not you. Will you marry me?'

In her agitation Dorothea jumped to her feet and clasped her hands over her reticule. 'Oh, but I cannot, sir, for what if the story got out? You would be the laughing-stock of London. I could not do that to you.'

'If that is your only reason for refusal, miss, then let me tell you it is a poor one,' he declared firmly. He reached for her hands and took them in his own after tossing her reticule aside on the bench. 'I want to marry you and my credit can survive any possible gossip from fools — not that there will be any. Now what do you say?'

'Your family will object.'

'Grandmother likes you and desires the match and my parents are dead. What other excuse can you find? Unless you really do not care for the idea.' His face grew bleak.

Unable to bear the change in his expression Dorothea cried out, 'Oh no! It is not that. I would like to marry you above all things but I am afraid you might suffer in the future for allying yourself to me.'

'The only suffering I have had of late is your refusal.'

'Was your pride very damaged, sir?'

'Yes, minx, it was, but far worse.' He tilted her chin up again. She saw the tender expression in his eyes and her own mirrored the same feelings. 'My heart suffered such a blow as I have never endured before. I had not realized how you had wormed your way into my thoughts and my life until you refused me and grew cold at every meeting.'

'You were just as distant and stiff,' she reminded him.

'I know. You caused a total loss of confidence in me, which is an unheard-of state. Now, my little love, will you say yes and marry me?'

'What did you call me?' she murmured shyly, gazing at him with adoration.

'My little love. Did you not guess I have loved you almost from that first moment when you fell at my wheels in a Derbyshire lane? It was the luckiest day of my life.'

'And mine.'

'Does that mean you care too?' he asked with incredulous hope.

'Oh yes. I thought you were the man of my dreams and I arranged for the family to come to London just so that I could see Mr Detherfield again. When I found out who you really were I thought there was no chance for me.'

'So you refused my offer. How silly can you be, my little love.' He bent his head and kissed her lips, tenderly at first then with growing passion as she responded to his embrace. They remained entwined for several minutes before he reluctantly drew away.

'My grandmother will send Maud in search of us in a moment, but before we go in there is something I want to give you.' He pulled out a slim jewel case from his pocket and handed it to her. When she opened it, Dorothea found it contained a diamond necklace like the one he had torn from Mrs Howard the night before.

'This is the real necklace which belonged to your mother. I bought it. I thought you would like it to remind you of her sometimes,' he said quietly.

'It's beautiful. I can hardly believe it was hers.'

'You should have had all the jewellery but that woman stole it and sold it. Never mind, I will buy you plenty more instead.'

'I would prefer what you buy me, sir.'

'Martin,' he corrected gently. 'No more Lord Rothley or sir, if you please. We are officially betrothed as from this moment and I intend to wed you as soon as I can. Now we had better find my grandmother and tell her our news.'

They strolled back to the house arm in arm. Lady Rothley appeared at the garden door and waved her stick at them. 'Took your time about it, lad. No life in you young sprigs now. Come along. I want my luncheon.'

Laughing, they went together into the house.

We do hope that you have enjoyed reading this large print book.

Did you know that all of our titles are available for purchase?

We publish a wide range of high quality large print books including:
Romances, Mysteries, Classics
General Fiction
Non Fiction and Westerns

Special interest titles available in large print are:
The Little Oxford Dictionary
Music Book
Song Book
Hymn Book
Service Book

Also available from us courtesy of Oxford University Press:
Young Readers' Dictionary
(large print edition)
Young Readers' Thesaurus
(large print edition)

For further information or a free brochure, please contact us at:
Ulverscroft Large Print Books Ltd.,
The Green, Bradgate Road, Anstey,
Leicester, LE7 7FU, England.
Tel: (00 44) **0116 236 4325**
Fax: (00 44) **0116 234 0205**

THE DUKE'S REFORM

Fenella J. Miller

Devastated by the deaths of his wife and daughters, Alexander, the Duke of Rochester, vows never to love again. Drinking and gambling numb the pain while he searches for a woman to enter a marriage of convenience and produce an heir. The beautiful Lady Isobel Drummond seems ideal for the task, and the union saves her family from financial ruin. But Alexander's high-handed and dissolute ways soon drive Isobel away, just as he acknowledges his growing feelings for her. Can he convince his beloved that he is a changed man? And can Isobel ever regain trust in the man she once loved?

VALERIE'S RUSSIA

Sara Judge

1913: An unexpected offer from the Empress of Russia, who seeks an English companion for her children, brings Valerie Marsh to the Alexander Palace at Tsarskoe Selo. There, she is torn between two cultures — and two passions: Pyotr Silakov, a handsome young cavalry officer in the Tsar's household; and Grigorii Rasputin, the Tsarina's holy man and friend. But Silakov, obliged to marry the rich and beautiful Sophia Lukaev, wants Valerie only for his mistress; whilst folk whisper that Rasputin is nothing but a lecherous charlatan . . . Meanwhile, the clouds of war loom on the horizon — what will become of Valerie when the storm breaks?

MISS DARCY'S PASSION

Wendy Soliman

When Dominic Sanford's parents die in a carriage accident, he is packed off to Scotland to be brought up in his uncle's household. Years later, he returns to his dilapidated estate that borders Pemberley. His father's journals have recently come into his possession, raising questions about his parents' deaths . . . Upon seeing Dominic for the first time at Colonel Fitzwilliam's wedding, Georgiana Darcy feels an immediate attraction. As she assists him in delving deeper into his family's history, they uncover a fiendish web of organised criminality. But Georgiana unwittingly plays a major role in the miscreants' plans — by involving her, Dominic has placed her directly in danger's path . . .